Lutes, viols and temperaments

Lutes, viols and temperaments

MARK LINDLEY, 1937-

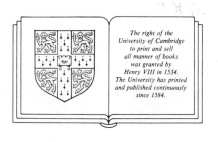

The right of the University of Cambridge to print and sell all manner of books was granted by Henry VIII in 1534. The University has printed and published continuously since 1584.

00028210

CAMBRIDGE UNIVERSITY PRESS

Cambridge

London   New York   New Rochelle

Melbourne   Sydney

Published by the Press Syndicate of the University of Cambridge
The Pitt Building, Trumpington Street, Cambridge CB2 1RP
32 East 57th Street, New York, NY 10022, USA
296 Beaconsfield Parade, Middle Park, Melbourne 3206, Australia

First published 1984

Printed in Great Britain at
the University Press, Cambridge

Library of Congress catalogue card number: 83-5171

British Library Cataloguing in Publication Data
Lindley, Mark
Lutes, viols and temperaments
1. Lute   2. Viol
I. Title
787'672   ML1010

ISBN 0 521 24670 9 hard covers
ISBN 0 521 28883 5 paperback
ISBN 0 521 26297 6 cassette

For Diana Poulton

Contents

Introduction

Tuning a lute or viol really well is not a simple matter of adjusting the open strings: one must also see to the exact spacing of the frets down the neck of the instrument. Some thirty players and theorists wrote about this problem between the 1520s and the 1740s. The key passages are here transcribed and translated and, when it is informative to do so, are analysed in relation to music of the day. I have made it a point to include some misleading theories of well-known authors, because it can often be as useful to know why one theorist should be dismissed as to know why another should be taken into account. My conclusions about performance practices are summarized in Chapter 7. Chapters 3 and 4 include fretting instructions for equal temperament and for two shades of meantone temperament. The index may be of use to readers with particular historical interests.

Chapter 1 explains that most of the various fretting methods which have been proposed for lutes and viols can be discussed under four broad headings:

pythagorean intonation, in which the 5ths and 4ths are untempered (tuned quite pure) and as a result most of the major 3rds and 6ths, including those among the open strings, are nearly 1/9 tone larger than pure,[1] and the diatonic semitones (those forming part of a diationic scale, such as C♯-D or A-B♭) are smaller than the chromatic ones (such as D♭-D or A-A♯);

equal temperament, in which the octave is made up of twelve equal semitones, and the 5ths and 4ths are slightly tempered, but much less so than the 3rds and 6ths;

---

1 Among the notes shown here, if the frequency of vibration for the G is 81 during every scant 1/4 or 1/5 second (which is the right range), then the C a pure 5th below will have a frequency of 54 (2/3 of 81); the F, 72 (4/3 of 54); and the B♭, 48 (2/3 of 72). But a pure major 6th above the B♭ would have a frequency of 80 (5/3 of 48); so the 81:48 major 6th is larger than pure by 81:80, which is slightly less than 1/9 of 81/72 (the whole-tone between G and F). The 81:80 discrepancy is called the syntonic comma.

81 : 54 : 72 : 48

meantone temperaments, in which the 5ths and 4ths are tempered rather more than in equal temperament so that the 3rds and 6ths will be only moderately tempered (indeed, the major 3rd may even be pure in one well-known form of meantone temperament), and the diatonic semitones are larger than the chromatic;

just intonation, in which not only most of the 5ths and 4ths are untempered, but also the major 3rd at fret 4 and between the two middle courses. Two sizes of whole-tone (9:8 and 10:9) and several sizes of semitone are involved. Also, if one of the open-string 4ths is not tuned some 1/9 tone larger than pure, the double octave between the first and sixth courses must be left smaller than pure by that amount.

Chapters 2-5 discuss each of these types in turn. Chapter 2 describes the pythagorean fretting schemes of some sixteenth-century writers, notably Oronce Fine (p. 10) and Juan Bermudo (pp. 13-18), who were no doubt impressed by its theoretical venerability and unaware that competent players of the day favoured a tempered intonation. Some lute music issued by Fine's publisher, Pierre Attaingnant, is examined in this light (pp. 12-13).

Late-renaissance theorists established that lutes and viols were normally set for equal temperament (unlike keyboard instruments), and composers ever since have assumed that they could be played in all keys without the extra frets which would theoretically be necessary for any system other than equal temperament. Chapter 3 complements this basic point with: evidence for the use of equal semitones on some fretted instruments before 1550 (pp. 19-22); a critical comparison of the $\sqrt[12]{2}$ and 18/17 methods (p. 21); an explanation of why early-sixteenth-century theorists described equal temperament obliquely (pp. 23-27); an analysis of relevant passages from Aristoxenus and Macrobius (pp. 30-31); a description of Bermudo's frettings for an approximation to equal temperament (pp. 27-30); a scheme for lutes invented by the first president of the Royal Society and based on the golden section (pp. 33-36); and finally, evidence from Michael Praetorius (pp. 36-37) and Marin Marais (pp. 38-41) that players could, without particularly altering the frets, make the instrument produce some kind of intonation other than equal temperament.

Chapter 4 explains the technical and musical characteristics of meantone temperament (pp. 43-45 and 51-54) and complements the last section of the preceding chapter with a survey of testimony from various late-sixteenth- and early-seventeenth-century writers (with particular attention to Giovanni Battista Doni) as to how well lutes and viols could match the intonation of keyboard instruments, which at that time were tuned to one or another of the various regular forms of meantone temperament (pp. 46-50). Chapter 4 also shows that two early-sixteenth-century composers, Arnolt Schlick and Luis Milán, probably intended their music for some shade of meantone temperament (pp. 51-58), and examines the fretting instructions of Hans Gerle (pp. 58-60) and Silvestro Ganassi (pp. 60-65): these are irregular schemes, but they may have served as pragmatic approaches to a meantone temperament. The chapter concludes with some practical fretting instructions.

Chapter 5 examines some representative schemes for just-intonation fretting (Mersenne is treated at some length) and explains why none of them have been taken beyond the experimental stage. Chapter 6 analyses the rather chaotic fretting instructions published by John Dowland, and shows that he himself never used them (pp. 81-83). Also, the 'modified meantone' for fretted instruments which J. Murray Barbour attributed to Giovanni Maria Artusi is shown to have been, in reality, a theory of equal temperament for vocal music, attributed implicitly to Claudio Monteverdi (pp. 84-92).[2] Chapter 7 summarizes the practical implications of the preceding six chapters.

Some ancillary topics are dealt with in the first three appendices. In Appendix 4 Gerhard Söhne shows how certain historical lute designs embody a fairly close matching of proportions and more complex geometric elements (mathematically not unlike the matching, for equal temperament, of 18:17 and $\sqrt[12]{2}$). The lute-makers and designers cited in Appendix 4 include Henri Arnaut, Matteo Sellas, Vvendelio Venere, Hans Frei, and as a counter-example – a distinguished maker whose designs resist mathematical analysis – Michielle Harton.

I should like to describe briefly here the criteria by which it can be shown that Dowland's music requires a more or less equal temperament, that the music of Schlick and Milán fits meantone temperament, and that the preludes published by Attaingnant are *not* suited to pythagorean intonation.

The only real test is the sound. On several occasions when I have tuned a suitable instrument in an historically likely manner and then tried out some part of the appropriate repertory for the first time, I have met with surprises; and always I have heard *something*, some effect in the harmony, some rapport between a nuance of the tuning and the instrument's timbre, which could not be anticipated from looking at the score. (Of course some composers have cultivated such subtleties less than others.) The tablature notation (explained in Appendix 1 for readers unfamiliar with it) does give us

---

2 Part of Chapter 6 appeared, in somewhat different form, in *Early Music History 2* (Cambridge 1982), 393-404, and an early version of part of Chapter 3 in *JLSA* XI (1978), 45-62.

some valuable clues. It allows us to determine whether the composer has called upon the same pair of frets for a diatonic semitone on one string and a chromatic semitone on another. If he has done so quite freely among the first few frets (where it is harder for the player to fudge the intonation) or between the nut and fret 1, a meantone temperament can be ruled out, because in that kind of tuning the substitution of a chromatic semitone for a diatonic one will usually produce a sour chord. On the other hand, if he has gone out of his way to avoid using the same fret for a diatonic and a chromatic semitone, particularly in the same composition, we may infer a sensibility to the limitations of meantone tuning. In the case of pythagorean intonation the issue is more elaborate: here the exchange of one size of semitone for the other may sometimes have a good effect, because the difference in size between the two kinds of semitone in pythagorean intonation is virtually the same as the difference between a pythagorean and a pure 3rd or 6th. As we look for a convincing pattern of distribution among the relatively pure and impure chords (and among the relatively dull and incisive semitones), we are led again to tune an appropriate instrument and discover the musical effect.

A certain kind of scholar will complain – indeed has complained[3] – that this method is too subjective, even when accompanied by the other kinds of evidence described here. I think it worthwhile, however, to use our ears as best we can, and hope for a well-informed consensus to confirm our perceptions, or improve upon them. To that end the publishers (to whom I am grateful for the care which they have lavished upon this little book) have distributed also a tape cassette with recordings of some of the examples from Attaingnant, Milán, Valderrabano, Louis Couperin and Marais. Each example on the lute is played twice, with different fretting schemes. The example from Louis Couperin complements Appendix 2 and supplies the necessary background for an appreciation of John Hsu's ability to match the harpsichord's tuning on the viol. Presumably Marais could do this as well.

3   So far I have received this complaint only from a scholar who had not heard the tunings.

1 Classifying temperaments

Any account of the history of tempered tuning on lutes and viols might well begin with an admission that even the best tuner cannot impose a theoretical scheme upon these instruments very exactly. For one thing players cannot help but alter, in greater or lesser degree, the tension and therefore the pitch of a stopped string when they press it down to the fret. Pietro Aron referred to this leeway when he said in 1545 that the lutenist's finger can aid the intonation of the instrument by the *intensione* and *remissione* of a minute space;[1] and Michael Praetorius in 1619 spoke of a 'give and take' in the string by which the player's grip at the fret of a lute or viol could mitigate the defective semitones of equal temperament (see below, p. 36). On a viol the pressure of the bow stroke can also modify the pitch.

Gut strings are in any case less uniform than metal. Their mass per unit length may vary so much that, as Hubert Le Blanc declared in 1740, 'Two strings of the same thickness, as clear as rock crystal, make the 5th at a considerably different degree forward and back.'[2] Fastidious players will discard strings which are altogether false (renaissance and baroque tutors show that this was a recurrent problem), but even the best gut strings will have some slight irregularity. It is part of their charm.

How far the player's leeway and the string's irregularity may go is hard to say, but certainly far enough to render it immaterial that a perfect 5th in equal temperament is theoretically smaller than pure.[3] The amount – two cents – is just enough for most keyboard-tuners to have to take it into account, but is too slight to be worth mentioning in practical instructions for the lute or viol. A knowledgeable pianist such as Johann Nepomuk Hummel will carefully specify the quality of the 5ths in equal temperament (1828):

---

1 Aron 1545: 35ᵛ.
2 Le Blanc 1740: 138.
3 In equal temperament all twelve 5ths are smaller and all 4ths larger than pure by 2 cents, or 1/12 of the pythagorean comma, the amount (theoretically 23.4 cents) by which a chain of twelve pure 5ths and 4ths will yield an impure unison or octave.

To afford the ear some guide respecting these flattened fifths, we may divide them into three species, into good, bad and absolutely perfect. A fifth is bad when it sounds too flat with regard to the lower note. It is good, when not indeed absolutely perfect, but yet so nearly so as not to sound offensive to the ear.[4]

But it would be idle to expect such finesse in tuning instructions for fretted instruments. Instead, the Burwell instruction book for the lute (c1670) says: 'Now one cannot well tune his lute unless it be well strung and have good fretts . . . the best way to place them [is] by the Eare Singing the Gamott . . . You must use several meanes for the accomplishment of so important a thing as the tuneing . . .'[5] Jean Rousseau (1687) says:

On peut accorder la Viole par Quartes, & c'est la maniere ordinaire des Maistres qui distinguent facilement la justesse de cét Intervalle en touchant deux chordes à l'ouvert. On peut encore accorder la Viole par Quintes & par Octaves, mais il est certain que la veritable maniere de bien accorder est de se servir de toutes ces manieres l'une après l'autre, comme d'un moyen infaillible pour connoistre le deffaut des chordes, pour y remedier quand la chose est possible, en avançant ou ritirant un peu les Touches.	One can tune the viol by 4ths, and this is the usual method of master players, who distinguish readily the proper tuning of this interval while playing two open strings. One can also tune the viol by 5ths and by octaves; but it is certain that the true method of tuning well is to use all these methods one after the other, as an infallible means for detecting faults among the strings, in order to remedy them (when that is possible) by moving the frets slightly up or down.[6]

Danoville (also 1687) is just as vague:

les Musiciens . . . par la justesse de leur oreille accordent toutes leurs Cordes à l'ouvert, & arrangent par ce moyen les Touches dans les lieux & places qu'elles doivent estre . . . Le plus facile & le plus aisé à pratiquer c'est celuy des unissons, les autres il les faut laisser pour les Musiciens.	Musicians by the trueness of their ears tune all their strings open and thereby arrange the frets where they ought to be . . . The easiest and most convenient [method] is that of unisons; the others must be left to musicians.[7]

In the sixteenth century, Ganassi (1543) and certain unnamed vihuelists referred to disapprovingly by Bermudo (1555) would also habitually refine the fretting by ear rather than adhere literally to any mathematical scheme (see below, pp. 60-65 for Ganassi and p. 18 for Bermudo).

All of which means that when we consider the various ways of tempering a lute or viol, we should avoid too minute a system of classification, and

---

4   Hummel 1827: 443 (1828: 70). Similar passages can be found in earlier writers, for example Rameau (1737: 101); Fritz (1756: 22); Marpurg (1776: 169).
5   The Burwell Lute Tutor: 7ᵛ-8ʳ; or see Dart 1958: 16-17.
6   Jean Rousseau 1687: 36-38.
7   Danoville 1687: 34 & 37.

favour a broader one allowing for vagaries of string tension during the playing and of mass per unit length in the string. It may be informative to reduce a fretting formula to a set of intervals calculated in cents, but it would be very naive to imagine that the frets will impose such an intonation of the scale upon the performance as definitively as the harpsichord- or organ-tuner's handiwork does.

Certain choices, however, do have to be made merely to get the open strings of a normal six-course instrument in tune. The syntonic comma – the amount by which four pure 4ths and a pure major 3rd fall short of two full octaves[8] – has to be distributed somehow among them. Presumably the double octave between the outer courses should not be compromised, at least not perceptibly. Should then the 4ths be made pure and the major 3rd left a comma larger than pure? This would imply pythagorean intonation. Or should all five intervals be 'stretched' the same amount, that is, by 1/5 comma each? This would be one form of meantone temperament. There are other possibilities: to stretch the 3rd by more than 1/5 comma and the 4ths less (as in equal temperament, for example); to tune the 3rd pure and stretch each of the 4ths by 1/4 comma (a well-known form of meantone temperament); to temper some 4ths more than others.

In due course the fretting scheme and tuning of the open strings must be coordinated. Everyone's instructions agree, for instance, that the open strings must make good unisons and octaves with stopped notes on the other courses. Ganassi is among those who specify that good octaves and unisons should govern the final adjustments of all the frets, as indicated in Example 1. Here one can see that frets 2, 4, 5, 7 and 8 are to be tested against open strings. On the middle strings fret 1 is adjusted for a good unison with fret 5. Then 3 and 6 have to provide a good unison or octave with 1. While the

Example 1. Some of Ganassi's tuning checks for the viol (1543: ch. 6). In the tablature notation (explained below in Appendix 1) each line represents one of the instrument's six strings. Ganassi presented the 1-3-1 and 1-6-1 checks melodically because to play them harmonically would make the left hand stretch too far, and because the 1-3-1 check involves non-adjacent strings that cannot be bowed in one stroke without touching the others between.

8   As explained in the note to p. 1, this amounts to 1/9 whole-tone (more exactly, $21\frac{1}{2}$ cents) and its ratio is $\frac{4}{3} \times \frac{4}{3} \times \frac{5}{4} \times \frac{4}{3} \times \frac{4}{3} \times \frac{1}{4} = \frac{80}{81}$.

open-string intervals and fret locations are thus mutually tested, no unison between 5 and 0 is overlooked, and we have seen that this particular habit is implicit in the instructions of other writers, such as Danoville and Jean Rousseau. So if the open 4ths are tuned differently in any systematic way, fret 5 should slant or zigzag accordingly. But since renaissance and baroque tutors never suggest this, we may assume for purposes of classification that the open 4ths are tuned alike. In which case, if the octaves are pure, the 5ths will also be alike.

Now, among the various 'regular' tunings – that is, theoretical schemes with uniform 4ths and 5ths – we may observe various salient characteristics which distinguish each type. Meantone temperament has major 3rds that are either pure or only slightly tempered, whereas equal temperament and pythagorean intonation have major 3rds that are distinctly larger than pure. Equal temperament has uniform semitones, but pythagorean intonation and the various shades of meantone temperament have unequal semitones. These characteristics will suffice to reduce most of the fretting schemes given in the various renaissance and baroque tutors to three reasonably broad types. Writers are usually explicit as to whether they intend equal or unequal semitones; the quality of the open-string 3rd can normally be inferred from the placing of fret 4. Table 1 shows how these criteria may be used to distinguish the three categories of regular tuning – pythagorean intonation, equal temperament and meantone temperament – which will be discussed in Chapters 2, 3 and 4.

Table 1. Classification of regular models of tuning and temperament for fretted instruments. The model represented by the empty space at the lower right (which would divide a pure or nearly pure major 3rd into four equal semitones) is discussed on p. 84 below.

fretting:	open courses	
	distinctly large major 3rd	approximately pure major 3rd
distinctly unequal semitones	*pythagorean intonation*	*meantone temperament*
functionally equal semitones	*equal temperament*	

2 *Pythagorean intonation*

Pythagoras is a somewhat legendary figure from whom no writings are extant and whose name has therefore been attached to various ideas he may perhaps never have dreamt of. The term 'pythagorean intonation' has traditionally been taken to refer not so much to a scale as to a way of reckoning or constructing intervals: the string-length ratios 2:1, 3:2 and 4:3 are used (for the octave, 5th and 4th), but no ratios involving 5 or any larger prime number are allowed. The normal ratio for a whole-tone is thus 9:8 (3:2 divided by 4:3, since the whole-tone is the difference between a 5th and a 4th). The ratio for a 'ditone' or major 3rd is $(9:8)^2$, that is, 81:64. This interval is a syntonic comma[1] larger than a pure major 3rd, for which the proper ratio is 5:4. By further calculations one may reach 256:241 as the ratio for a pythagorean minor 2nd or diatonic semitone (4:3 ÷ 81:64), and 2187:2048 for a chromatic semitone (9:8 ÷ 256:241).

The traditional term, from ancient Greek theory, for the diatonic pythagorean semitone is 'limma'; and for the larger, chromatic semitone, 'apotome'.

The oldest extant fretting formula, that of the ninth-century theorist Al-Kindī for the '*ud* (the Arabic lute), is pythagorean. It calls for five frets, to make the following succession of semitones down from the nut: limma, apotome; limma, apotome; limma.[2] In pythagorean schemes for the European lute or viol, one would expect frets 2, 4 and 5 to have the same positions, so that if the open-string note is *ut* in the traditional Guidonian hexachord, then those frets will give *re*, *mi* and *fa* respectively. Of course fret 7 (*sol*) will be 1/3 of the distance from the nut to the bridge. But where should we expect to find the 'chromatic' frets 1, 3 and 6? We shall find that different theorists gave different answers, particularly for fret 6.

When Pierre Attaingnant began to publish lute music in 1530, he

---

1 See p. 1 for a discussion of the syntonic comma.
2 Wright 1980: Table 1. According to Wright, fret 1 was a hypothetical addition not actually used. This is suggested by the Arabic names of the other four frets, which mean 'first finger', 'middle finger', 'ring finger', and 'little finger'.

10

published also a brief 'epitome' of music theory by Oronce Fine. Fine was a fairly accomplished engraver as well as a humanist and mathematician (in 1530 or 1531 he became Professor of Mathematics at the new Royal College in Paris), and for the *Epithoma musice instrumentalis*[3] he made a woodcut of his fretting scheme for the lute (Figure 1). In this scheme each 'chromatic' fret is placed in the lower half, musically, of the whole-tone which it divides. Fine also included a monochord scheme of the same description (Figure 2).

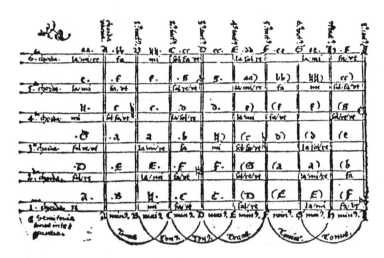

Figure 1. Fine's fretting scheme (1530). The open courses, reading from the bottom up, are named A, D, G, ♭, e and aa.

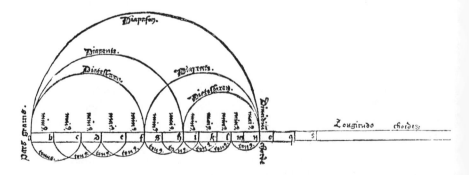

Figure 2. Fine's monochord diagram (1530). Going up from the *pars gravis* at the left, the semitones are labelled: minus, maius, minus, maius, minus; minus, maius; minus, maius, minus, minus, maius.

3   A copy of this short work, with unnumbered pages, is in the Österreichische Nationalibiliothek at Vienna.

Thus he not only duplicated Al-Kindī's fretting but also conformed to the fifteenth- and early-sixteenth-century European tradition of monochord theory, exemplified in treatises by Henri Arnaut (*c*1440), Johannes Legrenze (*c*1465), Nicola Burzio (1487), Franchino Gafurio (1496), Heinrich Schreiber of Erfurt (1514) and Pietro Aron (1516). All of these agree that the minor semitone 'precedes' the major and is to be placed in the lower or left-hand part of the whole-tone.[4]

A generation after Fine, the anonymous *Discours non plus melancoliques que diverses, de choses mêmement qui appartiennent à notre France* put fret 6 closer to 7 than to 5:[5]

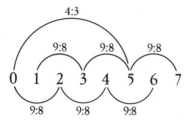

There is reason, however, to doubt the practical significance of any sixteenth-century pythagorean scheme. As far as I have been able to tell from contemporary evidence, Fine was not really a musician,[6] and one might suspect as much of the author of the *Discours non plus melancoliques que diverses* since that work deals with all sorts of non-musical matters. More important, it happens that several sixteenth-century theorists who were practical musicians, including Gafurio (1518), Giovanni Spataro (1521), Giovanni Maria Lanfranco (1533), Aron (1545) and Thomas Morley (1597), confused pythagorean intonation and meantone temperament by using a pythagorean model of the scale to describe one of the salient characteristics of meantone temperament on keyboard instruments: the fact that D♯ and G♯ differ from E♭ and A♭.[7] Finally, we shall see in Chapters 3 and 4 that there is plenty of evidence in sixteenth-century treatises for the use of tempered tuning on fretted instruments.

4 Lindley 1980a.
5 *Discours*: 101-04. For a depiction of this fretting scheme on a lute, see Figure 27 below. A copy of the *Discours* is in the British Library, Hirsch Collection I 593. I am indebted to Ian Harwood for showing me this, and for being generally helpful in the preparation of this book.
6 According to *The new Grove*, Attaingnant 1529 is but an earlier version of Fine 1530; the correct spelling of the name is Finé, and he was 'reputedly an excellent lutenist'. Heartz (1964: xvii) contradicts the first assertion (and I agree); Hamm 1975 and Poulle 1978 spell the name 'Fine' (and Poulle explains why); and none of these (nor any primary source known to me) yields any evidence that Fine played the lute at all. Poulle concludes (1978: 156): 'It appears that the goal of his publications, which ranged in subject matter from astronomy to instrumental music, was to popularize the university science that he himself had been taught.'
7 Lindley 1975-6.

To complement (or else to refute) that evidence I selected a representative sample of Attaingnant's lute music – the preludes which he published in 1529 – and listened to them repeatedly in various tunings.[8]

The first prelude sounds surprisingly well in pythagorean intonation with Fine's fretting. The counterpoint is so restless here that the pythagorean growling of the 3rds and 6ths is fairly innocuous (Example 2*a*).[9] A moment of nice chromatic shading, where I have placed an asterisk, is made particularly sweet by a paradoxical feature of the tuning: fret 1 is closer to the nut than to fret 2 by just enough to give a virtually pure major 3rd with fret 2 on the next lower course when the open 4th is not tempered larger than pure. (In one sense the interval might be spelt E-A♭ since it is derived, as far as the tuning is concerned, from the chain of pure 5ths and 4ths, A♭-E♭-B♭-F-C-G-D-A-E; but it is used here, of course, as a major 3rd, that is, E-G♯.) One might hardly guess from looking at the music that the momentary purity of E-G♯ will in fact grace the leap to C (which itself is intoned rather low in

Example 2. Attaingnant, Prelude 1 (1529), excerpts.

8 Attaingnant 1529 or Heartz 1964 (where the transcriptions are a whole-tone lower). Concerning the alphabetic tablature notation, see Appendix 1 below.
9 To my ear, however, the C♯ towards the end of this excerpt sounds too high in pythagorean intonation.

relation to E); but it is easy to imagine that this same pure G♯ will be re-markably appropriate when it occurs at the conclusion of the piece (Example 2*b*).

The same tuning sounds well enough for most of the second prelude as well; but this time the concluding triad contains a B that beats profusely and distractingly (Example 3). So also does the C♯ which is dwelt upon not far into the third prelude (Example 4). Finally, in Example 5, an excerpt from the fourth prelude, the triads and major 10ths want a certain solidity which is too conspicuously lacking in pythagorean intonation. Nor is the pure G♯ placed here with any particular cunning, as it occurs at a moment of urgency rather than repose.

On balance, therefore, it seems doubtful to me that sensitive players would really have left the pythagorean scheme unaltered.

Juan Bermudo, however, did sometimes use pythagorean intonation. Although chapters 75-86 of the fourth book of his *Declaración de instru-mentos musicales* refer to the vihuela rather than the lute, I should like to discuss them here because of the importance of the vihuela repertory and be-cause I believe their content and significance have often been misunder-

Example 3. Attaingnant, Prelude 2 (1529), conclusion.

Example 4. Attaingnant, Prelude 3 (1529), beginning.

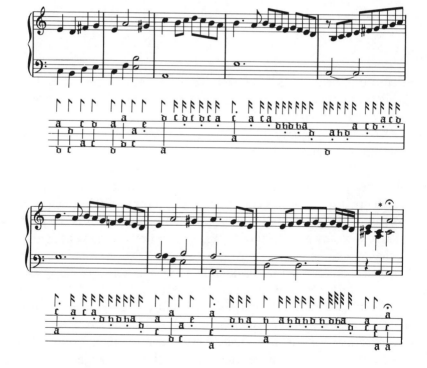

Example 5. Attaingnant, Prelude 4 (1529), excerpt.

stood.[10] Apart from two methods for approximating equal temperament (discussed in Chapter 3 below), Bermudo gave various fret arrangements for pythagorean intonation, but he was, as we shall see, evidently unable to hear the difference between this kind of tuning and meantone temperament as practised on contemporary keyboard instruments. I shall outline the general course of his discussion so that his various arrangements of limma and apotome among the frets can be kept track of properly. He used the terms *mi* and *fa*. A *mi* fret is for notes that normally have a diatonic semitone above them in the chromatic scale – in other words, E and B and any sharps – whereas a *fa* fret is for notes, like F and B♭, with a diatonic semitone below them.

Bermudo's fundamental precept was that the frets should never be adjusted by ear. He established this premise in a special paragraph, set in large type, just before chapter 75:

Para el curioso tañedor	For the attentive player.
Resta para los musicos curiosos dar	It remains to give, for attentive musicians,
artificio de poner los trastes	a method of placing the frets
por compas en la vihuela:	on the vihuela by means of a compass.
y quedara mas perfecta, por	This will be more perfect, because
ser mas cierto el compas, que el oydo.	the compass is more certain than the ear.[11]

Chapter 75 is devoted to the first and more rudimentary of the two methods for equal semitones. Chapter 76 announces a new seven-course vihuela of Bermudo's own devising, in which the tuning would be facilitated by having

---

10 Bermudo 1555: 101ᵛ-111ʳ. Among various examples of misunderstanding which could be cited, perhaps the silliest is that of John Ward, whose discussion of this material is based on the premise that 'though 16th-century vihuelas were fretted for a kind of equal temperament, all semitones were not equal; the *mi* frets were a comma higher than the *fa* frets' (1953: 32-33).
11 Bermudo 1555: 101ᵛ. *Compas* does mean 'compass'.

no 3rds or 6ths among the open courses: Γ-C-F-G-c-f-g. Chapter 77 gives a pythagorean fretting for this new instrument, in which fret 3 is set for a pythagorean *fa* (that is, closer to 2 than to 4, just as in the schemes of Al-Kindī and Fine) but frets 1, 6 and 8 are set for a pythagorean *mi*. Chapter 78 discusses some of the virtues of this arrangement and is followed by an illustration of it (see Figure 3), but the same chapter also presents some alternative methods for the chromatic frets, with fret 3 giving a pythagorean *mi* while 1, 6 and 8 give *fa*. Chapter 79, however, continues to dwell upon the virtues of the first arrangement. The following excerpts show how Bermudo confused his pythagorean *mi* and *fa* with the equivalent notes on contemporary keyboard instruments, which were (unbeknownst to him) tuned in meantone temperament, as a wealth of evidence from other theorists, including Ramis de Pareja (1482), Martinez de Biscargui (1528 . . . 1550), Tomas de Sancta Maria (1565) and Francisco de Salinas (1577), confirms.[12] The technical details in the second half of this passage can be grasped readily by referring to Figure 3:

Ya que auemos tractado la perfection de la vihuela de siepte ordines: es bien que veamos si la dicha vihuela tiene alguna imperfectiõ . . . Presupongo como cosa cierta, que la tecla negra de entre Gsolreut y	Now that we have treated the perfecting of the seven-course vihuela, it would be well to see whether the said vihuela has any imperfections . . . I presuppose as a certainty that the black key between G and

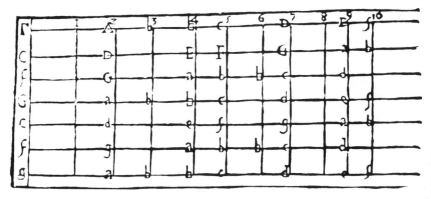

Demõftraciõ dela vihuela de fiete ordenes

Figure 3. Bermudo's pythagorean fretting for his seven-course vihuela (1555: 104[r]). The open courses, reading from the top (visually), are named Γ, C, F, G, c, f and g.

12 Ramis 1482: 80-81; Biscargui 1528: ch. 27 (1550: ch. 28); Sancta Maria 1565: ch. 53; Salinas 1577: 143-64.

alamire antiguamente era fa y ahora sirue	A was formerly *fa* but now serves
de mi . . . en algunos monachordios	as *mi* [although] in some harpsichords
de Flandes viene la dicha tecla	from Flanders the said key occurs
demanera, que forme fa y mi . . .	in a way that forms [both] *fa* and *mi* . . .
Tractemos primero las faltas que	Let us treat first the faults which
parecià enel traste tercero.	might appear [to be] at the 3rd fret.
En la cuerda quinta y en la segunda	On the fifth and second strings
enel tercero traste dixe ser fa, y	I said a *fa* is at the 3rd fret; yet
auia de ser mi para corresponder al	it might have to be *mi* to match the
organo. Este no es deffecto . . .	organ. This is not a defect because
en el octavo en la sexta y en la	at the 8th [fret] on the sixth and
tercera estan mi, y	third [strings] there are *mi*s, and
assi mesmo en la quarta y en la prima	similarly on the fourth and first
enel traste primero forma mi . . .	[strings] *mi* is formed at the 1st fret.[13]

Chapters 80 and 81 present various pythagorean fretting schemes for
normal six-course vihuelas, that is, with a major 3rd between the two middle
courses (the other courses being a 4th apart). If the outer courses are named
G or C, the same fretting as described in chapter 77 is to be used. If they are
named F, then all the chromatic frets are to be *mi*, but if they are named B,
then even fret 4 will be *fa*; and so on for a total of five different fretting
schemes as outlined in Table 2. The next chapter confirms the importance
which Bermudo must have attributed to all this, by inveighing at some length
against the use of slanted frets and irregular strings. In contemporary practice the use of slanted frets may have had to do rather with meantone tem-

Table 2. The relation between Bermudo's choice of nomenclature for the
open strings on a normal six-course vihuela and his choices as to whether
frets 1, 3, 4, 6 and 8 should be for *mi* or *fa* notes.

if the outer courses are named	then fret			
	3	1	6	4&8
	should be set to give			
F	*mi*	*mi*	*mi*	*mi*
C or G	*fa*	*mi*	*mi*	*mi*
D	*fa*	*fa*	*mi*	*mi*
A or E	*fa*	*fa*	*fa*	*mi*
B	*fa*	*fa*	*fa*	*fa*

13 Bermudo 1555: 104^r-104^v.

perament than (as Bermudo thought) with pythagorean intonation; but here anyway is a sampling of his admonitions:

A los curioses con toda instācia	To attentive [readers], with all solicitation
suplico, que noten dos puntos.	I request that they take note of two points.
El primero que las sobre dichas	The first [is] that the above-mentioned
faltas algunos pretenden remediarlas	faults some [people] pretend to remedy
con poner los trastes	by putting the frets
donde estan las dichas faltas	(where the said faults occur)
a costados, sacādolos del quadrado.	at a slant, deflecting them from a right angle.
Do por exemplo el traste primero	I give as an example the 1st fret
dela vihuela de gamaut, el qual es	of the vihuela in G, which is
mi para quatro cuerdas, y auia de	*mi* on four [of the] strings and [yet] has to
ser fa para la tercera y segunda.	be *fa* on the second and third [strings].[14]
. . . Lo segundo que se deue notar	The second [point] to be noted
es vn error nopequeño que	is a considerable error which
entre algunos tañedores de vihuela	among some players of the vihuela
se practica cada dia. Dizen	is practised every day. They say [that they]
auer cuerdas subidas de tono,	have [some] strings raised in pitch
y otras baxas de tono . . .	and others lowered in pitch . . .
Son estas cuerdas semejantes alos	[But] such strings are like
christianos malos de secrete, que	surreptitiously bad Christians who
non parece su maldad.	conceal their sins.[15]

Chapter 83 advocates the adoption of fixed frets on the six-course vihuela, including double frets, a comma's worth apart in each instance, for frets 1 and 4. (The *mi* alternative is to be slightly less thick so as not to buzz against the string when the *fa* is being used.) Several references to the organ in the following vein confirm that Bermudo perceived no distinction between his pythagorean style of intonation and the contemporary style of keyboard instruments (which were actually tuned in a meantone temperament):

si el primero en Cfaut	If the first [mode] transposed to C
por el organo tiene bmol,	on the organ requires the flat
correspondiente al fa de bfabmi;	corresponding to the [dorian] B♭,
no tiene tecla negra donde se ponga.	there is no black key where it is to be.
Esta boz de bemol tenia a	This flat note [A♭ in C minor] belongs to
la tecla negra de entre Gsolreut	the black key between G
y Alamire, y esta es mi.	and A, but that [key] is a *mi* on the organ:
Luego en ella no puedan formar fa.	hence *fa* cannot be formed by it.
Esta vihuela de la gamaut tiene	[But] this G vihuela has
el dicho fa en la quarta	the said *fa* on the fourth [string]
en el tercero.	[i.e. the F course] at the 3rd [fret].[16]

Chapter 84 is quite brief and intended to prepare us to appreciate the importance of Bermudo's new and rather sophisticated method for equal temperament, which is set out in chapter 86. The intervening chapter (85) is devoted to pythagorean schemes for the guitar and bandurria.

14 That is, on the D and A courses fret 1 has to provide E♭ and B♭, while on the G, C and F courses it has to provide G♯, C♯ and F♯.
15 Bermudo 1555: 107ʳ-107ᵛ.   16 Bermudo 1555: 107ᵛ-108ʳ.

3 Equal temperament

Most theorists between 1550 and 1650 regarded lutes and viols as equal-temperament instruments. In some treatises this feature was cited to under-score the categorical distinction between fretted instruments and keyboard instruments, which at that time used some form of meantone temperament. The list of theorists includes such major figures as Vicentino, Zarlino, Salinas, Artusi, Praetorius and Mersenne;[1] and probably all composers of the late renaissance and since have assumed that fretted instruments are not sub-ject to the limitations of a meantone temperament. Once this basic point has been acknowledged, the main questions of interest to historically minded players concern the status of equal temperament before c1550, and the extent to which players since then may have used their instruments' re-sources of flexibility to depart from the theoretical norm of equal tempera-ment, for the sake, perhaps, of more euphonious 3rds.[2]

Was equal temperament used as a fretting scheme before 1550? Frets spaced for equal semitones seem to be depicted in works of art as early as the fifteenth century, for example Lorenzo Costa's well-known portrait of a lutenist, now in the National Gallery in London (Figure 4). But a work of art may undergo so many vicissitudes of retouching and the like, and indeed may originally have been made for so many reasons other than to render ex-actly the normal spacing of frets on a contemporary lute or viol, that the pic-torial evidence needs to be supplemented with other kinds of information. As it happens, however, there is some oblique but nonetheless persuasive evidence in writings from the first half of the sixteenth century to the effect that semitones amounting to 1/12 octave were indeed being used on some fretted instruments.

---

1 Vicentino 1555: 103^r & 146^v; Zarlino 1571: 221, and 1588: 197; Salinas 1577: 143-75; Artusi 1600: 35^v; Praetorius 1619: 65-66 & 150-58; for Mersenne, see pp. 76-79 below.
2 While 4ths and 5ths in equal temperament are tempered by only 2 cents (see Chapter 1, note 3), each major 3rd is tempered, larger than pure, by 14 cents or 1/3 of the 'lesser diesis' (theoretically 41 cents), the amount by which three pure major 3rds will fall short of an octave.

Figure 4. Lorenzo Costa (formerly attributed to Ercole de' Roberti), Concert (London, National Gallery).

Early-renaissance theorists denied categorically the possibility of equal semitones. Their non-existence was 'proven' by explaining that if a whole-tone of ratio 9:8 were divided into two semitones of ratio 18:17 and 17:16, then obviously one of them (18:17) would be smaller than the other. Hence the term 'minor semitone', though often applied to the pythagorean limma (256:241), could also refer to the interval with the 18:17 ratio.[3] But this is

3   See Boethius, *De institutione musica*: book III, ch. 1 (1491 edition: 186); Ptolemy, *Harmonika*, book I, ch. 10 (1562 edition: 68); Marchetto 1784 edition: 75; Clercx 1955: 59 (on Ciconia); Prosdocimo 1913 edition: 745-46; Anselmi 1961 edition: 89; Legrenze 1876 edition: 321-22; de Podio 1495: 24^r; Zarlino 1571: 165-66; Cardano 1663 edition: 107, and 1570: 170 (both passages translated below).

the ratio prescribed by Vincenzo Galilei in 1582 to mark off the frets down the neck of the lute for equal temperament, to which in fact it is likely to give a better approximation than $\sqrt[12]{2}$, because the latter figure makes no allowance for the fact that pressing the string to the fret increases its tension and so yields a higher pitch than the change in length alone would lead one to suppose. To compensate for the increased tension the string should be just slightly longer, and in fact the 18:17 method gives a better result. (On a tenor lute it renders the string at fret 12 longer by an amount – some 1/3 of 1% – comparable to the width of a double fret.)[4] So Vincenzo Galilei was perfectly sensible to recommend the 18:17 rule, with a pragmatic qualification:

auuertisco l'industrioso agente che con la sua discrezione & diligenza cerchi ouuiare a quella poca disconuenienza, che è tra il misurante & il misurato.	I advise the industrious agent that with his discretion and diligence he seek to obviate that slight discrepancy that there is between the measure [the 18:17 rule] and the [ideal theoretical distance] measured.[5]

Mersenne reported in 1637 that the 18:17 method was used by 'plusieurs Facteurs' of the lute (the passage is translated on p. 77 below).

In this light it is proper, I think, to find evidence for equal temperament in certain sixteenth-century references to the use of minor semitones on the lute. The mathematician Girolamo Cardano, who probably played the cittern and lute, wrote in his *De musica* (first drafted *c* 1546):[6]

tonus consistit in proportione sexquioctaua . . . & dimidium quodquod consistit in proportione 18. ad 17. & vocatur semitonium minus	A whole-tone consists in the proportion 9:8, and either half consists in the proportion of 18 to 17 and is called a minor semitone.[7]

In a later book on numerical proportions (1570) Cardano said, in reference to the 18:17 and 17:16 semitones:

Hic subit admiratio quomodo semitonium minus aptet tam gratem in symphonijs, maius autem nequiquam.	It is wonderful how the minor semitone is so nicely suited to to musical performance, but the major [one] never.[8]

---

4 My own experience is confirmed by Jahnal 1962: 150-53; he discusses the physical reasons why 'The rule of the old masters [18:17] sounds rather good to the ear up to the octave fret, whereas the ''theoretical rule'' sounds more and more ''false'' the closer we approach to the octave fret.'
5 Vincenzo Galilei 1581: 49. Zarlino did battle with Galilei and targeted this statement for particularly wry criticism (1588: 203).
6. Miller 1973: 17-19.   7 Cardano 1663 edition: 107.   8 Cardano 1570: 170.

In the fourth edition of his *Musica instrumentalis deudsch* (1545), Martin Agricola said that:

. . . fast das gröste part	Nearly the majority
Der Lautnisten und Geiger art	of lutenists and fiddlers
Alle bünd machen gleich von ein.	make all the frets equal.

. . . ein bund	. . . A fret
Der Semiton minus/thut kind	marks out a minor semitone.[9]

While this implies that not everyone used equal semitones, it says that those who did would space their frets a minor semitone's worth apart - which would make sense only with the 18:17 type. Even more telling is a remark attributed to Marc Antonio Cavazzoni by Giovanni Spataro, in a letter of 1524, that 'the lute has small semitones for all its frets' ('el leuto ha tuti li soi tasti semitonii minori').[10] The topic of this letter was Willaert's composition *Quid non ebrietas*, which goes through the circle of 5ths and ends with an octave between D and E♭♭ (see below, Appendix 2).

Some examples of less esoteric music implicitly requiring equal temperament are Enriquez de Valderrabano's pieces, published in 1547, for two vihuelas pitched a minor 3rd apart.[11] There is no way that these compositions could sound in tune on normal instruments in meantone temperament or pythagorean intonation.

The beginning of Nicola Vicentino's chapter (1555) on the 'defects' of fretted instruments will serve to complete the evidence which I have cited from Cardano, Agricola, Cavazzoni and Valderrabano for the use of equal temperament before 1550:

Dichiar. sopra li difetti del Liuto,	Statement on the defects of the lute,
e delle Viole d'arco, et altri	viols, and other
strometi cõ simili diuisioni.	instruments with similar divisions [of the scale].
C. LXV	Chapter 65.
Dall'inuentione delle viole d'arco,	From the invention of viols
et del Liuto fin hora	and the lute until now,
sempre s'ha sonato con	they have always been played with
la diuisione de i semitoni pari . . .	the equal-semitone division . . .[12]

Before taking up the question of whether players may have used their instruments' resources of flexibility to obtain less heavily tempered 3rds and

---

9 Agricola 1545: 53ᵛ-54ʳ.
10 Biblioteca Vaticana MS lat. 5318: 213ʳ-214ᵛ, transcribed and translated in Lowinsky 1956-8: 17. Regarding Lowinsky's surmise that 'If Cavazzoni wrote that the frets of the lute were all placed in intervals of minor semitones, then he expressed himself inaccurately', see the sources cited in note 3 above. For Ludovico Fogliani (to whom the letter was addressed), 16:15 was a minor semitone 27:25 major (1529: 19ᵛ).
11 Valderrabano 1547: 48-50. One of these duets is transcribed in Pujol's 1965 edition: 54.
12 Vicentino 1555: 146ᵛ.

6ths from an equal-temperament fretting, it will be worth our while to review some of the intellectual challenges which confronted renaissance theorists of tempered tuning. This will show why it was difficult for writers before the late sixteenth century to describe equal temperament very clearly, and put us in a position to appreciate the ingenuity of Juan Bermudo's imperfect solution to the problem. It will also show why late-sixteenth-century advocates of equal temperament made such a *cause célèbre* of Aristoxenus, and why some theorists, once it did become possible to give an exact mathematical formulation of equal temperament, went to such extraordinary lengths, quite beyond the needs of any musician, to elaborate upon the achievement.

In their attempts to describe contemporary tuning systems, renaissance theorists had to overcome the venerable authority of Boethius (d. AD 524), the most influential figure in the history of Western music theory. It was Boethius who had secured the position of music in the medieval 'quadrivium' of mathematical disciplines, which he classified according to their subject matter as follows:[13]

continuous quantities: magnitudes	discrete quantities: multitudes
stable magnitudes: *geometry*	multitudes *per se*: *arithmetic*
rotating magnitudes: *astronomy*	ratios between multitudes: *musical science*

This rather precludes the posibility of considering musical pitch as a continuum, so it is perhaps not surprising that Boethius was content to take the 18:17:16 model as proof that equal semitones were an impossibility.[14]

Boethius also said that the comma was the smallest intervallic quantity which could be heard[15] – a vague remark, but one which some renaissance theorists cited uncritically or even embellished into a theory that the comma was a 'minimum and indivisible' quantity.[16]

The doctrine of unequal semitones was challenged only after a geometric method for finding the proportional mean between two string lengths became available in 1482 with the publication of a Latin translation (by a thirteenth-century scholar, Johannes Campanus) of Euclid's *Elements*.[17] Theorists like Jacques Lefèvre d'Etaples (1496) and Heinrich Schreiber of

---

13 Boethius, *De arithmetica*: book I, ch. 1.
14 Boethius, *De institutione musica*: book III, ch. 1.
15 Ibid.: book III, ch. 10.
16 Bermudo 1555: 102^r ('Dixo Boecio, que la minima distancia que en la Musica se siente: es la coma'); de Podio 1495: 24^v-25^r ('Coma est spacium, sonum omnium minimum atque indivisibilium').
17 *Preclarissimus liber elementorum Euclidis* . . . (Venice, 1482). Palisca (1967: 638) cites an edition at Augsburg the same year.

Erfurt (1518) showed how this method could be applied on the monochord to divide a pythagorean whole-tone into two equal semitones (Figure 5).[18] The same device might be used to divide the octave itself into two, four, eight, sixteen (etc.) equal parts – but not twelve, as that would require dividing one musical interval into *three* equal parts. It was not until 1558 that a music theorist, Gioseffo Zarlino, described another ancient device – the 'mesolabe' – for finding theoretically any number of mean proportionals

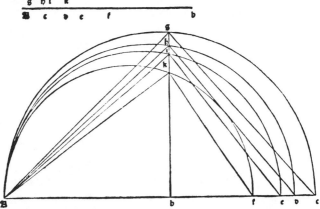

❡ **Tonum et octm confonantiam fimplicem:in duo equa partiri/veraɋ medictatum 35 puncta in chorda:geometrice monftrare.**

❡ Precedentes feptima ſcdilʔ viceſſimatertia tertiṷ pretedũt tonũ/diateſſaron/ diapēte ac diapaſon: in duo equa diuidi non poſſe.hecˣo mõſtrat quo pacto ea omnia poſtint in duo equa partiri.nec hoc quidẽ repugnat.Ńã p:eccedetes contẽuunt id effici non poſſe Brithmetice certo ʹcõſtitutoɋ numero/ atɋ ratiċali habitudine:hec ˣo id effici poſſe geometrice fine numeri certa/cõſtantiɋ ratione.

g b i   k
β   c   ꝺ e   f   b

❡ Sit ergo data chorda a b fuperior in qua iubeamur integrum femitonium/et pʃcnãtiarũ diateſſa ron/diapente/ac diapafon vera media reperire.facio a b 7 cb tonum.a b et d b diateſſaron. a b 7 e b diapente.a b et f b diapafon co qui in preteditbus mẽſtratus eſt meto.deinte in inferiori linea a c intcfinite quãtitatis capio a b equale linee fuperiori a b et b c ;tinue equalem linee b c fuperiori.et a puncto b verſs c:capio lineam b b equalem choite b d et b c equale choide b et b f choide b f.et in: telligo ãttuor dimidice circulos a c/a d/a e/a f.et a puncto b cduco perpẽticulare linee a c ad circũ : ſcrẽtes ſemicirculorũ a c a d/a e/a f.et r ũcta vbi cce cõtingit linea ſint g, b/i/k:at que ; ũcta educo a g/c g/a b/d b/a i/e i/a k/f k.at per nonã ſexti geometrice a b ad b g vt b g ad b c.facio igit in chorda fupertore a b lineam b g equalẽ inferiori linee b g et cũ ꝓpoitio a b ad g b vt g b ad c b vt p:eoſtẽſum eſt:ſedtur tenum a b 7 c b eſſe in tuo equa diuiſi.m:7 pũctũ g eſſe medium veri femitonu ſignũ.et per eãdem que,ꝓpoitio a b ad b b ea ſit b b ad b b.eſto igitur b b in chorda a b equalis linee b b per idem vt piius:ea crit,ꝓpoitio a b ad b b queb b ad b b.Quare a b et d b diateſſaron in tuo equa partita eſt. et eedem pacto facta chorda i b fupcriori equali linee b i.et chorda k b equali linee b k: mõſtrabis cõ:

Figure 5a.

Figure 5. Demonstrations by the mathematicians Lefèvre (1496) and Schreiber (1518) of how the pythagorean whole-tone can be divided into equal semitones on the monochord, using 'Euclid's method for finding a mean proportion between two lines, by describing a semicircle upon the sum of the lines taken as diameter and then erecting a perpendicular at the juncture of the two lines' (Barbour 1951: x).

The proof is fairly simple: If we drew the triangle ACD it would, being inscribed in a semicircle, make a right angle at C (according to another Euclidian theorem), so the angles ACB and DCB would complement each other. Since the angle ACB would also be complementary to CAB, and DCB to CDB, the triangles ABC and DBC would have the same angles and therefore would be similar, from which it follows that BA:BC::BC:BD.

18 Lefèvre 1496: book III, 35; Schreiber (alias Henricus Grammateus) 1518-21: Miij[v].

¶ Ayn zuſchꝛeiben die ſemitonia minoꝛa.
¶ Iſt zu mereck ain yeꜩlicher ton⁹ wirt getailt
jn ſemitoniū mai⁹ vñ min⁹ Alſo nym die zꝛwo li⸗
nten welche tonum geben vnd thue ſie zuſamen
Darnach ſuche dz mittel jn welchs ſeꜩ den ꜩir⸗
ckel mit dem ainen fuß vnnd ſpann den andern
Bis an das endt der linien vud ſchꝛeyß ain halbē
circkel Nach dem zeuch mit dem winckelmaß
ain linien vom punct wu die zwo linien ſein zu⸗
ſamen gethon biß zu dem Bogen oder halbenn
circkel/vnnd die ſelbig leng nym mit dem circkel
vnd ſeꜩ den aynen fuß jn das b/ vnd der ander
kegen dem a ſagt das punct woue dañ iſt ain zu⸗
ſchꝛeibē der ſemitonium minus Darnach mach
zwey kleyn halß circkel die richt auff jm a vnd b
zeuch dar uber ain ſayten ſo iſt alle ding Bereit.

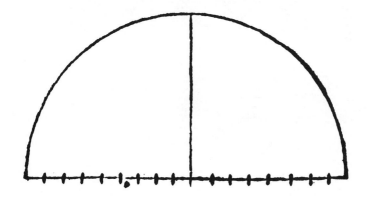

Figure 5b.

between two given lengths.[19] It consisted of a set of identical rectangular frames which could slide horizontally between two parallel rails and overlap one another. Zarlino later published several geometrical methods for laying out a lute in equal temperament, one of which is shown in Figure 6; and this kind of thing became something of a game among learned theorists well into the seventeenth century. (An account of the mesolabe and of some other, simpler devices is given below in Appendix 3.)

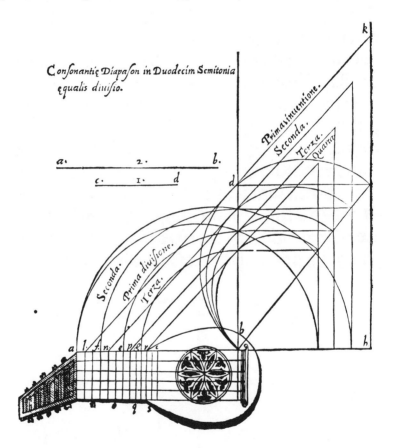

Figure 6. One of Zarlino's methods for fretting a lute for equal temperament (1588: 211). This method integrates Lefèvre's simultaneous application of the Euclidian method to more than one interval (see Figure 5) with an analogous expansion of a method by Philo of Byzantium for finding two mean proportionals.

19 Zarlino 1558: 94-96. The 'theorem of two mean proportionals' was of some importance in the ancient Greek technology of catapults (see Marsden 1971: 274), but its musical application seems to have been a renaissance idea.

No less awkward than finding equal semitones on the monochord was the concept of fractions of a comma. It was quite alien in 1496 to Gafurio, who regarded 5ths on the organ (in some form of meantone temperament) as being diminished by merely 'a small and hidden amount'.[20] In 1529 Ludovico Fogliani, imagining that the comma on a monochord might be divided in two by the Euclidian method (see Figure 7), said that practical musicians used a D tempered by 1/2 comma in relation to a justly intoned C and E (which was true in 1/4-comma meantone temperament) and to G and A as well (which was not the case).[21]

It is fascinating to observe the elaborate and slightly irregular procedure by which Bermudo split the comma rather more finely than this in the fretting scheme which he prescribed for equal temperament in book IV, chapter

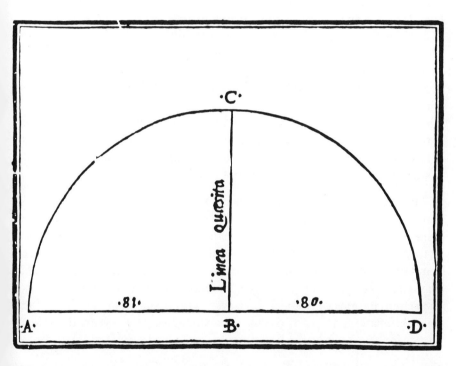

Figure 7. Fogliani's application of the Euclidian method to the division of the syntonic comma (1529: 36^r). AB and BD represent the string lengths for two pitches a comma apart, and BC represents the length for a pitch halfway between them musically.

The exercise is of purely theoretical interest, since the difference between this and the pitch produced by a string length of $80\frac{1}{2}$ is only 1/30 of a cent – that is, $(\log\frac{80\frac{1}{2}}{80} - \frac{1}{2}\log\frac{81}{80}) \div \frac{\log 2}{1200} = \frac{1}{29.9}$.

20 Gafurio 1496: book III, ch. 3, rule 2. See apropos Lindley 1975-6.
21 Fogliani 1529: 35^v.

16 of his *Declaración* (1555; see Figure 8). Though intended primarily for his new seven-course vihuela, the method was, Bermudo said, suitable for all fretted instruments and contained whole-tones that would enable an organ to play all the semitones.[22] Starting from the nut, frets 5, 10, 3 and 8 form a pythagorean succession; but then frets 2, 4 and 6 are placed virtually as in equal temperament. Here is a step-by-step summary of Bermudo's procedures:

Fret 4 is 1/3 of the distance from a pythagorean to a 4:5 position. (In theory, for equal temperament it should be 1/3 of the distance intervallically, but the distinction between the arithmetic and geometric fracturing of a mere comma is quite inconsequential musically, so Bermudo's rule entails no real compromise in precision.)

Fret 2 is midway between pythagorean positions with the nut and with fret 4. Thus the whole-tones from the nut to fret 2 and thence to fret 4 are each 1/6 comma smaller than pythagorean.

Fret 6 is 1/3 of the distance from a pythagorean position with 4 to a 4:5 position with 2. Hence the relation of 6 to 2 and 4 is rather like that of 4 to the nut and 2.

There remain frets 7, 9 and 1. These are pythagorean with 2, 4 and 6 respectively. Fret 7 is thereby left about two cents' worth towards the nut from a theoretical equal-temperament position, but the discrepancy is too slight to obscure Bermudo's intention.

This method of Bermudo's is probably easier to execute, though harder to remember, than the 18:17 method. At the same time it is more accurate than the simple 'anti-Boethian' alternative of dividing the whole-tone of a pythagorean scheme in half arithmetically, that is, into 18:17 and 17:16 semitones. That formula, later prescribed for fretted instruments by Pablo Nassarre (1723),[23] was rejected by Bermudo as needing refinement to make the semitones musically equal. However, with the proviso that each of the four chromatic frets (1, 3, 6 and 8) be shifted slightly toward the bridge,

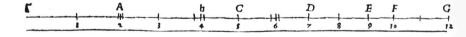

Figure 8. Bermudo's equal-temperament fretting scheme (1555: 109^v). The open string is named Γ (Gamma), and frets 2, 4, 5, 7, 9, 10 and 12 give the notes A, ♭, C, D, E, F and G.

22 Bermudo 1555: 109^r.   23 Nassarre 1723: 462.

Bermudo did accept it in chapter 75 (that is, near the beginning of his discussion of fretting) as a preliminary method 'for those with little knowledge':

Para poner en medio destos trastos	To place amidst these frets [2, 4, 5, 7, 9]
otros que formen semitonos, que seran	the others which make semitones – i.e.
primero, tercero, sexto, y octauo:	the first, third, sixth and eighth –
tomad este auiso.	follow this advice.
En medio delos trastes	Midway between the frets
que forman tono	which form a whole-tone
poned vno:	place one [fret]:
. . . Se el tono	. . . if the whole-tone
en la vihuela se diuidiera	were divided on the vihuela
en compas de arithmetica:	arithmetically,
facil cosa fuera poner los	it would be an easy thing to place the
trastes medios. Pero esta diuision	intermediate frets. But this division
no seria la mitad del tono	would not be the middle of the tone
por compas de Musica . . .	intervallically:
para hazer estos	to make these
trastes medios venir a tener el	intermediate frets occur at the
medio del tono	middle of the whole-tone
en compas de Musica:	intervallically,
aueys de quitar al	you have to subtract from the
medio que esta ala parte superior	upper half
vna poca de distãcia, y darsela ala	a slight distance and give it to the
parte inferior: y desta manera	lower part, and in this manner
quedaran los dichos trastes quasi	the said frets will be virtually
en medio en compas de musica.	at the middle intervallically.
Este arte de entrastar vihuelas no	This way of fretting vihuelas does not
va puntualmente en toda la perfectiõ	reach precisely all the perfection
que puede yr: . . . Puse lo aqui	that might be reached. I put it here,
en el lugar primero, y en modo no primo:	first in location but not in value,
para los que savan poco, y	for those with little knowledge, and
por comẽçar de lo imperfecto	to begin from imperfection
a imitacion de naturaleza.	in imitation of nature.[24]

Chapter 76, immediately following, expresses a slightly kinder opinion and, in passing, shows that Bermudo regarded equal semitones as normal for the common vihuela:

Los que los trastes de tono tienẽ	Those who keep the whole-tone frets
cõplido el tono, y	at the full whole-tone and
las diuisiones diuiden medio al	divide the divisions in half at
medio poco mas, o menos	[exactly] half (neither more nor less)
el dicho tono: estos son	[of] the said whole-tone: they are
dignos de ser alabados, y al	worthy to be praised, and the
inuentor del tal primor de major	inventor of this above all of greater
alabança. Realmente	praise. Really

24 Bermudo 1555: 102^r. According to Barbour (1951: 135), 'Bermudo, whose one tuning method was identical with Grammateus', did depend upon Faber for the method of constructing the mean proportionals'; but in fact Bermudo did not cite Lefèvre in this particular context.

en la vihuela cõmun no ay	on the common vihuela there are no
semitono mayor, ni menor: pero	major nor minor semitones, but
quedan ambos en tal disposicion:	both are so disposed
que se puedan tañer.	that they can be played.[25]

Most late-renaissance theorists (though not Zarlino)[26] associated equal temperament with Aristoxenus (third century BC), that disciple of Aristotle whose usual epithet among later Hellenic writers was 'the *musicus*' (*ho musikos*).[27] It was his theory of equal semitones which had provoked Boethius to declare them an impossibility. A brief look at the relevant parts of Aristoxenus' *Harmonika Stoicheia* will show that its renaissance readers (a Latin translation of sorts was published in 1562)[28] might well confuse equal temperament with some vague concept of pythagorean intonation, in much the same way that players did when they set out their frets for equal temperament without having in mind any explicit mathematical alternative to the traditional pythagorean ratios. A *locus classicus* for this confusion might be found in the following passage from Macrobius' *Commentary on the 'Dream of Scipio'* (AD *c*400), which was published in dozens of fifteenth- and sixteenth-century editions:

Symphonia *dia tesseron* constat de	The harmonic interval of a 4th consists of
duobus tonis et hemitonio,	two and a half whole-tones,
ut minutias quae additamenta sunt	(not to create difficulty, we leave out
relinquamus, ne difficultatem creemus,	some minute amounts which should be added),
et fit ex epitrito: *dia pente* constat	and is made from 4:3. The 5th consists
ex tribus tonis et hemitonio,	of three and a half whole-tones,
et fit de hemiolio: *dia pason* constat	and is made from 3:2. The octave consists
de sex tonis, et fit de duplari.	of six whole tones, and is made from 2:1.[29]

Aristoxenus had said that while we contemplate the musical functions of the notes by our intellect, we judge the magnitudes of the intervals by ear,[30] and therefore the very idea that height and depth of pitch consist in certain merely numerical ratios, or indeed ratios of vibrations, is extraneous to the subject of harmony.[31] He regarded the consonances as so many intervallic magnitudes (which might be taken to imply that he had particular sizes in

---

25 Bermudo 1555: 102ᵛ.
26 Zarlino 1571: 165-66 and 1588: 163; Vincenzo Galilei 1581: 42 & 53 (this was one of several points of disagreement between Zarlino and his former pupil); Artusi 1603: 32 (the passage is translated on p. 92 below); Doni 1647: 30 (according to Doni, equal temperament was 'commonly but erroneously' attributed to Aristoxenus).
27 Anderson 1980: 85.
28 At Zarlino's instigation (see Palisca 198-).
29 1848 edition: 137-38.
30 Aristoxenus 1562 translation: 23 ('reducitur totum negotium ad duo, ad auditum, scilicet & cogitationem. nam illo indicamus interuallorum magnitudines hac facultates eorum contemplamur'); Macran translation 1902: 189.
31 1562 translation: 29; Macran 1902: 198-99.

mind), and he remarked that in certain tetrachords the extremes were fixed a 4th apart regardless of the genus (diatonic, chromatic or enharmonic).[32] Yet he also allowed that concords need not be inflexibly determined in magnitude, but could perhaps suffer an 'inappreciable' degree of variation[33] – which seems to me a remarkable anticipation of one aspect of the idea of tempered tuning.

Aristoxenus derived the whole-tone as the difference between a 5th and a 4th; the major 3rd as twice that amount; and the semitone as half. Like everyone else at the time, he regarded 3rds and 6ths as discords; and he said that because the ear is more assured of the magnitudes of concords than of discords, the most accurate way to ascertain a major 3rd is by a chain of 5ths and 4ths (that is, going away a 4th, back a 5th, away another 4th and back another 5th).[34]

To a lutenist or viol-player, the practical message to be inferred from all this is fairly clear: Do not take the ratios very seriously; do not tune by 3rds or 6ths; set the 5ths and 4ths by ear and adjust them 'inappreciably', if need be, for the sake of equal semitones. Thus ancient authority could be cited in support of modern practice (equal temperament) at a time when science was, as yet, too weak to overcome the traditional metaphysical objections to the concept of equal semitones.

Equal temperament is even more strongly suggested in Aristoxenus' elaborate proof that a 4th consists of five semitones, particularly as the proof confirms that the whole-tone is exactly twice the size of the semitone difference between a 4th and a major 3rd. But here one of the key phrases was, unfortunately, reduced to nonsense in the 1562 translation.[35]

I might observe that a proper theoretical calculation of the pitch frequencies for a scale in equal temperament will adhere for the most part to Aristoxenus' exclusion of ratios, because the mathematical formulation of all the intervals except the octave is done with 'irrational' numbers (numbers which cannot be expressed as a ratio between two integers; in this case roots of 2).[36] Indeed, on plucked instruments, where the first overtone has in fact a

32 1562 translation: 29 & 34; Macran 1902: 199 & 206.
33 1562 translation: 34 ('Quia uero interuallarium magnitudinem, quae quidem consonatiis affines sunt, aut alioqui locum [variationi] habere non uidentur, sed in magnitudine terminata sunt, aut omnino simplicem quendam'); Macran 1902: 206. The 1562 translation is less than a model of clarity.
34 1562 translation: 35; Macran 1902: 207-08.
35 Loc. cit. ('cum excessus sit toniaeus & in aequalia diuisus, quorū utrumque sit Semitonium & excessus quidem ipsius Diatesseron est supra Ditonum, liquet quod quinque Semitoniorū continget esse ipsum Diapente [*recte* Diatesseron].'
36 Some roots of integers are themselves integers, like the square root of 9 or the cube root of 8. However, those which are not integers cannot be expressed as fractions either. One can readily see why by taking the opposite perspective: if a, b and n are integers, then $(a\frac{1}{b})^n$ is bound to be frac-

frequency slightly more than twice that of the fundamental (due to the 'inharmonic' timbre), even the octave might as well be represented by an irrational factor, as Lord Brouncker did in the 1650s (see below). The distinction is of course purely metaphysical. In a real measurement – as opposed to an abstract formulation – one writes nowadays a decimal number with however many digits correspond to an appropriate degree of precision (as I have done in Table 3).

Table 3. Fret positions for equal temperament, calculated by two methods.

fret	% of string length down from the nut step by step to	
	$\sqrt[12]{1/2}$ of the former length	17/18 of the former length
1	5.6	5.56
2	10.9	10.8
3	15.9	15.76
4	20.6	20.44
5	25.1	24.86
6	29.3	29
7	33.3	33
8	37	36.7
9	40.5	40.2
10	43.9	43.54
11	47	46.7
12	50	49.64

Simon Stevin, who is said to have invented decimal numbers,[37] used this principle in his manuscript calculations for equal temperament in the mid 1590s;[38] and in the 1620s decimal numbers facilitated no end the development of common logarithms, which a German engineer, Johannes Faulhaber, used to calculate an equal-temperament fretting scheme published at Frankfurt in 1630.[39] For some reason Mersenne overlooked logarithms, but

tional. Of course there is nothing unreasonable or uncertain about these 'irrational' answers to root-extraction problems, just as there is nothing unwholesome or incomplete about fractional answers to division problems. It is just that the two categories are mutually exclusive.

37 Minnaert 1976, or (better) Juschkewitsch 1964: 363-65.
38 Stevin 1966 edition: 446. He set his monochord length at 10,000 and not 3600 or the like.
39 Faulhaber 1630: 162-63. An abbreviated translation of the title is: 'Engineer's school, first part, in which is shown how to solve [various problems] quite satisfactorily and swiftly by the logarithmic rule'. Common logarithms for the numbers from 1 to 20,000 were published by Briggs in 1624, and Faulhaber set his string length at 20,000.

in 1653 their use was combined, in a most extraordinary manner, with a radically 'geometrical' approach to equal temperament, in the appendix to an English translation of Descartes' *Musicae compendium*. The anonymous translator appears to have been William Brouncker (later chosen by Charles II to be the first president of the Royal Society).[40] His variants of equal temperament were probably intended for the lute (see Figure 9).

Brouncker described the $\sqrt[12]{2}$ scheme,[41] but preferred one of his own devising with fret 12 at 50.6% from the bridge to the nut (whereas in the 18:17 method it is at 50.4%).[42] He said that since 'wee doe judge of Sounds according to the Geometricall . . . Proportion', the string should 'bee divided according to a Geometricall, not Arithmeticall Progression'; so instead of starting from fret 12 at midpoint, he 'let the chord AZ . . . be divided at S, into Extream and Mean Ration; by 30.6. Elem. Euclid'. This renders the proportion AZ:AS equal to AS:SZ, so that AS is the geometrical or proportional mean between AZ and SZ, and if one could pluck AS (notwithstanding that it is the segment between the nut and the fret) its pitch would be equally far above that of AZ and below that of SZ, the interval in question being some 51 cents less than a pure major 6th. Setting AZ at 10 and knowing that $\frac{AZ}{AS}=\frac{AS}{SZ}$, Brouncker deduced algebraically that AS must be 6.180, or 61.8% of the total length, leaving 38.2% for SZ (which is indeed 61.8% of 61.8%). Here is a slightly simplified version of Brouncker's deduction:

If AZ $=$ b and AS $=$ a, then SZ $=$ b $-$ a.

We intend that $\frac{a}{b}=\frac{b-a}{a}$.

It follows that $a^2 = b^2 - ba$.

Now if we add $ba + \frac{1}{4}b^2$ to both sides: $a^2 + ba + \frac{1}{4}b^2 = b^2 + \frac{1}{4}b^2$,

we can isolate a from b by taking the square roots: $a + \frac{1}{2}b = \sqrt{b^2 + \frac{1}{4}b^2}$,

and hence see that: $a = \sqrt{b^2 + \frac{1}{4}b^2} - \frac{1}{2}b$.

So if b $=$ 10, then a $= \sqrt{100 + 25} - 5$,

and by calculating $\sqrt{125}$ we shall find that a $=$ 6.18.

Of course not even SZ would ever be plucked, as there are no frets so close to the bridge, but if 'AS, the Mean Proportional, bee divided into 17 equall Semitones, by 16 mean Proportionals', the semitones are only some 2% smaller than in the $\sqrt[12]{2}$ method, and Brouncker believed that this division 'doth give (without any . . . sensible difference) all the simple consonances'. If so, it seems to have been a lucky coincidence, for in another (admittedly

40 Dubbey 1970.   41 Brouncker 1653: 91.
42 Brouncker 1653: 34-39. If AZ:AS::AS:SZ, then both ratios must amount to 2:√5– 1 (the ratio for the 'golden mean'). Fret 12 will be at $(\frac{\sqrt{5}-1}{2})^{17/12} = 50.57\%$. In the 18:17 method it is at $(17/18)^{12} = 50.36\%$.

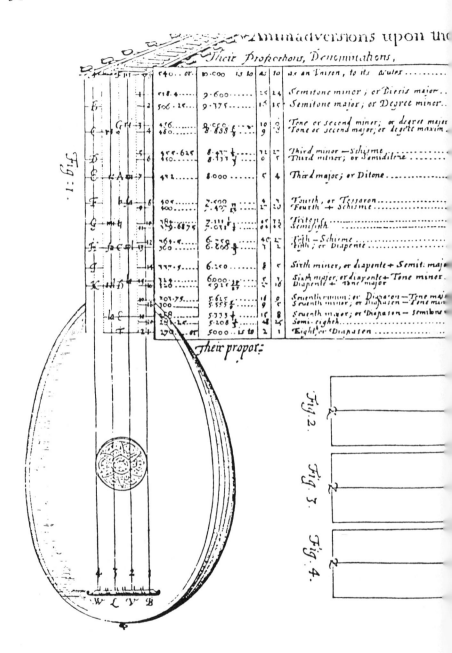

Figure 9. Brouncker's fretting schemes for a seven-course lute (1653:66-67). The left half deals with just intonation; the right half shows three schemes of equal semitones, placing fret 12 at 5.069, 5.000 and 4.941 respectively (from the nut to the bridge).

Musick-Compendium of R. des-Cartes

Differences.

		Differences.
1 2	Eighth, or Diapason	
	Semi-Eighth	Semitone minor, Diesis major, or Chromatica.
	Seventh major	Diesis minor, or Enharmenica. as 128. to 125. △
		Semitone minor.
	Seventh minor / Seventh minime	Schisma. as 81.to.80.△. as.81.to.80. ▽
		Semitone, or Limma Pythag. as 243.to 256. ▽
	Fifth + Second major / Sixth major	Schisma, or Comma major.
	Sixth minor	Semitone minor.
		Semitone major.
	Fifth / Fifth − Schisme	Schisme.
		Semitone minor.
	Semifth / Tritone	Comma minus. i.e. as 2048. to 2025. △
		Semitone minor.
	Fourth + Schisme / Fourth	Schisme.
		Semitone major.
	Third major	Semitone minor.
	Third minor / Third minor − Schisme	Schisme. } Semitone mod. as.135·128. △
		Semitone pythag. as.256. to.243. △
	Tone major / Second minor	Schisme.
	Semitone major / Semitone minor	Semitone minor. } Semit. max at 27 to 25. △
	at an unisone. to its graver.	Diesis minor. / Semitone minor.

ons, Denominations,   Differences.

less prominent) section of the appendix, Brouncker outlined another scheme – with semitones some $1\frac{3}{4}\%$ *larger* than in the $\sqrt[12]{2}$ method – starting from a point Q such that, in modern terms, the difference in frequency would be the same between ZA and AQ as between AQ and QZ ($\frac{1}{AZ} - \frac{1}{AQ} = \frac{1}{AQ} - \frac{1}{AZ}$), and then dividing AQ (58.6% of the AZ) 'into 15 equall Semitones'.[43]

These byways of music theory could make some glittering tiles in a mosaic portraying the infancy of modern science;[44] but for the musician and musical antiquarian I should now turn to the question of whether an equal-temperament fretting really implies the use of equal temperament in performance. Two distinguished seventeenth-century musicians, Michael Praetorius and Marin Marais, answered this question, obliquely but unmistakably, in the negative. Praetorius' answer is to be found in the following passage, at the words 'nehmen und geben kan' (which however were misprinted 'nennen und geben kan'):

vff den *Violen da Gamba*, vnd	On gambas and
den Lauten . . . die *Semitonia*,	lutes, the semitones
weder *majora* noch minora,	can and must be called
sondern vielmehr *intermedia*	'intermediate' much rather than
können vnd müssen genennet werden.	either 'major' or 'minor',
Sintemal meines erachtens	since, in my opinion,
ein jeder Bund . . .	each fret
$4\frac{1}{2}$. *Commata* in sich halten thut/da	marks off $4\frac{1}{2}$ commas, whereas
sonsten das *Semitonium majus*	otherwise the major semitone
fünff; das *Semit. minus* aber	[would] comprise
nur vier *Commata*	five and the minor semitone
in sich begreiffet.	only four commas.
Vnd weil dann nur ein halb *Comma*	And since only a half-comma then
an beyden theilen mangelt . . .	is lacking to each part,
vff . . . *Violen* vnd Lauten; (die an	on viols and lutes (which in
ihnen selbsten lieblich vnd still)	themselves [are] mild and quiet)
. . . kan der vnterscheyd nicht so	the discrepancy cannot be very
bald *observiret* vnd *deprehendiret* werden:	clearly observed and perceived,
Sonderlich/ weil man auch darneben	particularly since one also
den Saitten	can help give to and take from
mit den Griffen uff den Bünden	the string
helffen/ nennen vnd geben kan:	with one's grip at the frets.
Welches sich	This
in *Clavicymbeln*,	cannot be done at all
(do den Saitten)	with harpsichord strings

43   Brouncker 1653: 89.
44   A particular gleam would emanate from Isaac Newton's table (20 November 1665) with a colum in which the equal-temperament semitone ('an exact $\frac{1}{2}$ note') is employed as unit of measure t calculate the 'distance' of the notes in a just-intonation scale: 0.000000; 1.117313; 2.03910(3.156413; 3.863137; 4.980450; etc. These numbers can be converted to cents (invented b Albert Ellis nearly two hundred years later) merely by shifting the decimal point two places to th right. See Lindley 198–: §5.

vnd vff Orgeln (do den Pfeiffen	or organ pipes
nichts kan	where nothing can
zugegeben noch genommen werden:	be given or taken away,
Sondern bleiben müssen/ als sie	but they must remain as they
gestimmet vnd eingezogen seyn/)	are tuned and set.[45]
ganz nicht schicken wil.	

Seventy years later, some remarks by Marin Marais (in the continuo part-book to his first published work) show that an expert on the *basse de viole* could inflect the intonation of his instrument to conform with the tuning of a late-seventeenth-century French harpsichord. A detailed account of French harpsichord-tuning would be out of place here,[46] but to understand Marais' remarks one should know that while some theorists were already entertaining the ideal of equal temperament for keyboard instruments, harpsichordists were actually using an unequal temperament with the diatonic notes and F♯ approximating to some form of meantone temperament, most likely with the 5ths about 1/5 comma smaller than pure and the major 3rds thus about 1/5 comma larger. G♯ was tempered significantly more than 1/5 comma to E (being virtually pure with C♯), and two or three 5ths (A♭-E♭-B♭-F) were tuned slightly larger than pure, thereby dissipating the meantone wolf, which had normally been between G♯ and E♭. In addition, I am inclined to believe that C♯ was tempered less than 1/5 comma to F♯, and therefore more than that amount to A. In any case, the 3rds G♭-B♭-D♭-F-A♭-C, though generally worse than pythagorean (on account of the enlarged 5ths), could be used with impunity by a composer shrewd enough to turn their piquancy to good account, as Louis Couperin did in his famous F♯ minor Pavane (see Appendix 2).

While German writers like Andrea Werckmeister and Johann Philipp Bendeler were already working out monochord schemes to codify this new kind of keyboard tuning, French theorists said that its irregularities (vis-à-vis their quasi-scientific ideal of equal temperament) were due to some defect of the instrument or the tuner. At the same time, however, they acknowledged that these irregularities were so consistently distributed, from day to day and from one tuning to the next, that a musician could recognize the various keys by them. Thus Jacques Ozanam could assert, in 1691, that:

Quelque precaution que nous prenions	However much care we may take,
en accordant nos Instrumens	when tuning our instruments,
pour en rendre tous les Accords égaux,	to render all the intervals equal,
il ne laisse pas de s'y trouver toujours	there will inevitably be

45 Praetorius 1619:65-66.
46 See Lindley 198–: §6, or for a brief account 1980c: §§3 & 6.

quelque inégalité: & c'est ce qui fait que
nous remarquons un je ne sçai quoi de
triste ou de guay, de melodieux ou de dur,
qui nous fait distinguer un Mode d'avec
l'autre par le secours de l'oreille.
... C'est la même inégalité des
Intervalles semblables, qui faisoit
une des plus grandes differences
des Modes des Anciens ...

some inequality: and this makes us
notice a certain something of the
sad or gay, the melodious or harsh,
which makes us distinguish one key from
another by ear ...
Likewise, differences among
equivalent intervals might have caused
one of the greatest differences
among the modes of the Ancients.[47]

We should keep this context in mind when reading Marais' remarks of
1689. His first publication (1686) had consisted of suites in the perfectly
ordinary keys (for a *basse de viole*) of G, D and A major and D and G minor.
The volume of figured-bass parts to this music, published in 1689, included
some new pieces (in score, as it were) composed 'expressly for those who
have a great familiarity with the viol', some of them in G major or minor,
but others in the unusual keys of B and F# minor. At one point in his 1689
preface Marais said that the accompaniment might be played suitably on
either a harpsichord or a theorbo; but later, in discussing the F# minor
pieces in particular, he assumed that the accompanying instrument would be
a harpsichord, and I believe that only if we make the same momentary assumption can we understand the reason he gave for choosing the key of F#
minor:

je les ay toutes chiffrées, pour
les joüer sur le Clavecin, ou sur
le Theorbe; ce qui fait tres bien
auec la Viole, qui joüe le sujet.
On trouvera, a la fin de ces
Basse-continües, vne augmentation de
plusieurs Pieces particulieures ...
La premiere suitte que l'on trouvera
est composée sur le Dieze d'f,ut,fa,
qui est fort agreable sur la Viole,
et qui est assez en usage sur le Luth.
Ceux qui ne voudront pas se donner
la peine d'en joüer les Basse-
continües sur ce Ton transposé,
pourront aisement les joüer en
g,re,sol, un demy Ton au dessus:
et la Viole reglera son f,ut,fa# ,
sur le g,re,sol , du Clavecin.
On peut encor les joüer en a,mi,la,
du troisième Ton:
et demême il faudra

I have figured all the pieces for
playing on the harpsichord or on
the theorbo, which goes very well
with the viol, which plays the tune.
There will be found, following the
thorough-basses, a supplement of
several special pieces ...
The first suite to be found there
is composed in F# [minor],
which is very agreeable on the viol
and fairly commonly used on the lute.
Those who do not wish to take
the trouble of playing the thorough-
basses in this remote key
can easily play them in
G [minor], a semitone higher,
and the viol will take its F#
from the G of the harpsichord.
One can also play them in A
minor,[48]
and again it will be necessary

47 Ozanam 1691: 659-62.
48 Among contemporary French organ composers, for example Nivers (1675) and Boyvin (1675), the
troisième ton was represented by music in A minor – a tradition reflected by Jean-Jacques
Rousseau (1768: 519): 'Troisième Ton La mineur ou Sol'.

changer le Ton de la Viole.	to change the pitch of the viol.
La fantasie, qui est en b,fa,si,	The fantasy, which is in B [minor],
se peut de même transposer sur	can likewise be transposed to
le troisiême Ton: ce qui se peut	A minor – something that can be
faire sans embarras.	done without trouble.
Mais ces avis sont hors de Saison,	But these suggestions are untimely,
quand j'y pense, puisque	now that I think of it, since
presentement en France chacun	nowadays in France everyone
transpose si facilement sur tous	plays so easily in all
les Tons et Demi-tons.	keys however remote.
Enfin ie donne cet expedient	Thus I offer this expedient
pour ceux qui voudront	[merely] for those who will wish
s'en servir: car pour moy,	to make use of it. As for myself,
qui les ay composées sur le Ton	who composed them in the key
sur lequel on les trouvera,	in which they are to be found,
je les y aime beaucoup mieux que de	I like them much better there than
les transposer: parce qu'il se trouve	transposed, because there is
quelque chose de plus perçant dans	something more 'piercing' about
les Tons que j'ay choisy pour cela.	the keys that I have chosen for that purpose.[49]

The meaning of this last remark is oblique but, I think, unmistakable. As the strings of the viol would be more slack in F♯ minor than in the alternatives, the timbre of the instrument would actually be less piercing. Nor is Marais' adjective conceivably appropriate for the effect of the lower pitch level *per se*. If the music were played in equal temperament, which would be feasible with a theorbo but unlikely with a harpsichord in France at that time, the intervals in one key could not be more or less piercing than the equivalent intervals in another. There is no evidence that Marais was capable of romantically mystical notions (with no physical basis, that is) about the qualities of various keys.[50] This leaves only one likely explanation: that an expert viol-player accompanied by a harpsichord could match its intonation well enough – if for no other reason than to avoid capriciously sour unisons – to allow the relatively piercing quality of certain harmonies in F♯ minor on the harpsichord, for instance those involving the leading-note, to permeate the music.[51] At the beginning of the F♯ minor Suite, the leading-

---

49 Marais 1689: 2. See also Bol 1973: 92.

50 I have in mind a certain vein of late-eighteenth- and nineteenth-century thought. For example, in Heinse's novel *Hildegard von Hohenthal*, Lockmann says that A♭ major 'ist Majestät von König und Königin'; C. F. D. Schubart (1806) describes the same key as 'der Grabton. Tot, Grab, Verwesung, Gericht, Ewigkeit liegen in seinem Umfange'; while Beethoven describes it in a letter of 19 February 1813 (1907 edition: 123) as 'peu naturel et si peu analogue à l'inscription Amoroso, qu'au contraire il changerait en Barbaresco' (a quality I have failed to notice in the Adagio of his own 'Pathétique' Sonata). I am indebted to Rita Steblin for some of these references.

51 A possible exception should be considered for the 'pièces de clavessin' of Jean-Nicolas Geoffroy (d. 1694), preserved in a posthumously assembled manuscript (see Roche 1967: 40) in which no fewer than four suites are in new-fangled 'tons transposez' (and each has been copied, by the same hand, in a 'ton naturel': E→F major; A→G major; F minor→G minor; B minor→A minor). I have played these and find them not particularly well served by the irregular French style of unequal temperament.

note E♯ appears first in the bass line (bar 2) and then in a 6-chord (bar 3) rather than a chord upon C♯, which would have been rather harsh so early in the suite. The slow introduction is full of such niceties, the sequences being particularly elegant to the ear when the viol does adhere well enough to the harpsichord's intonation to capture its flavour (Example 6).

Even without a viol one can easily, on a harpsichord tuned in the French

Example 6. Marais, F♯ minor Suite (1689), opening (facsimile).

manner,[52] play the minuet from this suite in F♯ minor and in G minor to compare the effect of its sequences in the two contexts (Example 7).

Beyond Marais and F♯ minor in particular, the broader conclusion to be drawn from all this is that a master of the *basse de viole* could indeed be expected to make significant inflections.

Would such a master be likely to adjust the frets themselves to a slightly irregular spacing, with perhaps fret 4 (the most obvious candidate for change) closer to the nut than would be ideal for equal temperament? Perhaps so; but I dare say not beyond his capacity to make the unisons and octaves pure when playing – nor enough to produce any untempered 3rds. For that we have Rameau's word. Referring to the viol, he wrote in 1737:

on sçait que les deux Cordes moïennes   we know that the two middle strings
ut & *mi* forment entr'elles une   C and E form between themselves a

Example 7. Marais, F♯ minor Suite (1689), minuet, transcribed here for keyboard in F♯ minor and (the beginning) in G minor.

Tierce majeure trop forte, & qui	major 3rd [which is] too wide and which
doit l'être d'un Comma, dès que	must be so by a comma if
les Quartes sont justes d'ailleurs;	the 4ths are, for their part, pure;
aussi les Maîtres fortifient-ils,	hence the masters [of the viol] widen,
autant que l'Oreille le peut souffrir,	as much as the ear can bear it,
toutes les Quartes, pour que	all the 4ths, so that
la Tierce majeure puisse en être	the major 3rd might be
diminuée d'autant:	thus made smaller [than pythagorean].
nous tenons ce fait de M. Dequai	We have this fact from M. Dequai,
Ordinaire de la Musique de Sa Majesté.	his majesty's *Ordinaire de la Musique*.[53]

This suggests that the open-string 4ths were tempered quite perceptibly, which is really more than in equal temperament. Yet it seems reasonable to suppose that M. Dequai had a finer ear for these nuances than most of the rest of us, and hence that the amount of tempering was less than the same statement would imply in a manual for dilettantish players.

53   Rameau 1737: 90.

4 Meantone temperament

A number of scholars have used this term to refer to one particular scheme in which the 5ths and 4ths are each tempered by 1/4 comma – or some $5\frac{1}{2}$ cents – so that the major 3rds will be pure. (Of course if C-E and E-G♯ are pure, then the diminished 4th G♯-C, though it looks like a major 3rd on the keyboard, will be larger than the major 3rds by some 41 cents, the amount by which three pure 3rds would fall short of an octave.) But the traditional term 'sistema participato' included tunings in which the major 3rds were themselves slightly tempered, and the 5ths and 4ths were, accordingly, tempered less than 1/4 comma (or in one or two unusual schemes, more), as shown in Table 4. These are all 'regular varieties' of meantone temperament in that the 5ths in each type are uniform.[1] The 5ths are tempered at least twice as much as in equal temperament, however, and thus on a keyboard instrument with twelve notes per octave there will be one wolf 5th, larger than pure, at G♯-E♭ (or perhaps C♯-A♭ or D♯-B♭). Figure 10 below shows how the semitones of a twelve-note scale differ in meantone and equal temperament and pythagorean intonation (labelled 'B'). Notice that in meantone temperament (and this is true of all its regular varieties) the diatonic semitones, for instance E-F, are larger than 1/12 octave. This means that in any diatonic scale the leading-note is tuned lower in meantone than in equal temperament.[2]

Since keyboard instruments were normally tuned in some form of regular meantone temperament throughout most of the sixteenth century and at least the first part of the seventeenth, one would like to imagine that the

---

1 They are discussed in Barbour 1951: 32-42; Lindley 1980c; and Barbieri 198–. For historical justification of these scholars' application of the term 'meantone' to schemes with tempered major 3rds, see Sauveur 1707 ('il faut prendre *un* ton moyen', etc.) and Estève 1755 ('Le ton moyen étant au semi-ton comme 3 à 2, on formoit le systeme de 19. Le ton moyen étant au semi-ton comme 5 à 3, on formoit le systeme de 31. Le ton moyen étant au semi-ton comme 7 à 4, on formoit le systeme de 43', etc.).

2 According to Mersenne (1637b: 23), musicians of his day found equal temperament 'fort rude', partly 'à raison de . . . la diminution des demitons'!

most sensitive and adroit players of the lute or viol might accommodate their intonation to meantone for a more euphonious ensemble when accompanied by keyboard instruments. We should not be too optimistic about this, however. Vicentino said in 1555 that when lutes or viols played with instruments that had the whole-tone divided unequally, they were never quite in tune together ('Mai schiettamente s'accordano quando insieme suonano').[3] In the late 1570s Giovanni de' Bardi of the Florentine Camerata wrote to Giulio Caccini:

piu fiate mi è venuto voglia di ridere,	More than once I have felt like laughing
videndo strafelare i Musici per	when I saw musicians struggling to
bene unire viola, o liuto con	put a lute or viol into proper tune with
instrumento di tasti . . .	a keyboard instrument . . .
fino a questo giorno	Until now
non anno avvertita	this highly important matter
cosa di tanta importanza,	has gone unnoticed
e se avvertita, non rimediata.	or, if noticed, unremedied.[4]

In 1599 Ercole Bottrigari spent several pages of his *Il desiderio* discussing the intonational discrepancies between fretted and keyboard instruments.

Table 4. Tempering of triadic concords (stated in fractions of the syntonic comma) in various regular tuning systems. Each variety of meantone temperament is named after the amount by which its 5ths and 4ths are tempered (5ths smaller than pure, 4ths larger). Four times that fraction, plus the fraction by which the major 3rd is tempered (larger than pure) makes the full comma. The major 6th is tempered by the sum of the amounts for the 4th and the major 3rd.

	5ths & 4ths	major 3rds	major 6ths & minor 3rds
2/7-comma meantone	2/7	− 1/7	1/7
1/4-comma meantone	1/4	0	1/4
2/9-comma meantone	2/9	1/9	1/3
1/5-comma meantone	1/5	1/5	2/5
1/6-comma meantone	1/6	1/3	1/2
equal temperament	1/11	7/11	8/11
pythagorean intonation	0	1	1

---

3   Vicentino 1555: 146^v.
4   Published in Doni 1763b: 244, and translated in Strunk 1950: 297.

His quantitative grasp of meantone temperament was inadequate to his pur-
pose, but the underlying distinction between the two systems of temperament seems reasonably clear. In 1637 Mersenne, in a discussion of equal
temperament, after reporting that

selon le prouerbe commun	according to the common saying
des Praticiens, le Luth est	of musicians, the lute is
le Charlatan de la Musique,	the charlatan of music,
parce qu'il fait passer pour bon	because it passes off as good
ce qui est mauvais	that which is bad
sur les bons Instrumens . . .	on good instruments . . .

went on to declare it 'certain' that

l'Orgue & l'Epinette estans	if the organ and harpsichord were
temperées selon le manche	tempered according to the fretting
des Luths & des Violes,	of lutes and viols,
les concerts que en reussiront,	performances in which they are combined
paroistront plus justes, raison de	would seem more in tune, because
la conuenance de leurs accords . . .	their tuning would agree.[5]

In the 1660s an anonymous English writer, after (mistakenly) attributing to
John Berchinshaw a twelve-note pythagorean scheme with the wolf 5th
between G♯ and E♭, went on to say:

I am sure, and will prove it by any Organ, or Harpsichon, that is tuned only by the Eares of a well prac-
tized Musician, that there will be found a greater difference between such an Organ, and this
pythagorean Scale, then between the same Organ, and a Scale, which divideth an Eighth into twelve
equall Semiton's, which division all our Violls, Lutes, Gitares, and the like instruments doe follow . . .
An Organ so tuned will come nearest of all to that meantone division, which I have fitted for the
monochordon . . . The difference betwixt an Organ tuned by the Eares only, and the equall division is
very easily discerned by any bodies Eares; much more will the difference between the said Organ and
Mr Berchinshaw's Scale be perceptible. For the better understanding of which, I have drawn here three
lines, to represent the three several Scales, vz M mine, E the equall, and B Mr Berchinshaw's [Figure
10]. Not to be understood, as three strings but by equall parts representing equal Musicall intervalls.[6]

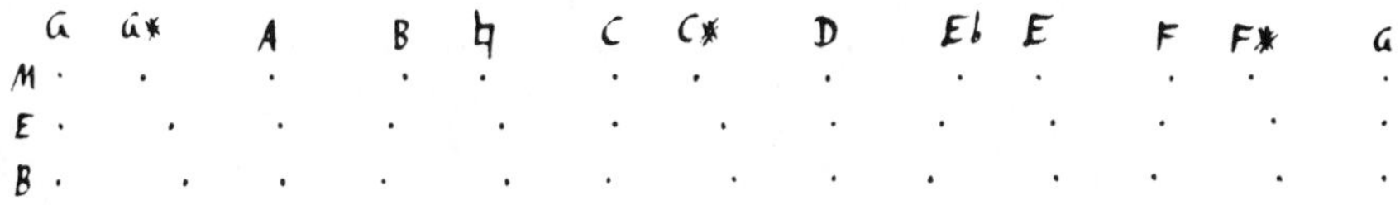

Figure 10. Relative sizes of semitones in three kinds of regular tuning (Birch Collection: British Library
Add. MS 4388, 43ʳ). Among the note names 'B' means B♭. The first row of dots, labelled 'M', must
represent a regular meantone temperament, but the exact shade is unspecified. The second row ('E') is
for equal temperament. The third row ('B') shows the anonymous author's selection of twelve notes from
John Berchinshaw's 34-note pythagorean scheme.

5 Mersenne 1637b: 20.
6 British Library, Birch Collection, Add. MS 4388: 42-43.

Clearly this all suggests that the ability to play a lute or viol in meantone temperament was unusual. A few writers between 1550 and 1650 do refer to some systematic arrangement of unequal semitones on fretted instruments, but nearly always in a manner which shows that practically no one used them. When Vicentino described in 1555 the ubiquitous use of equal semitones on fretted instruments and the fact that they never sounded in tune with keyboard instruments, he recommended the adoption of a scheme with the unequal semitones in the following order (opposite to the normal pythagorean pattern, but appropriate to meantone) for the first five frets: major, minor; major, minor; major. Similarly, in this dialogue from the second edition of Vincenzo Galilei's *Fronimo* (1584) the pattern of major and minor semitones in the musical illustration conforms to that of meantone temperament and excludes pythagorean intonation:

Eu. Vorrei sapere per qual cagione	*Eumatio*: I would like to know why
voi non vsate nel vostro Liuto . . .	you don't use, on your lute,
i tasti . . . distanti vno dall'altro	frets spaced
par in solita inegualità d'interualli,	to give unequal intervals,
& alcuni altri tastini, che	and some additional little frets to
tolgono alle terze & decime maggiori	take from the major 3rds and 10ths
parte dell' acutezza loro, come ho	some of their acuteness, as I have
ueduto vsare ad alcuni . . .	seen used by some [players] . . .
Fro. Risponderò prima	*Fronimo*: I shall deal first
all'inegualità de tasti . . .	with the inequality of the frets . . .
voi deuete sapere, che	You should know that
altra è la distributione del Liuto,	the lute's scale is different from
altra quella dello strumento di tasti	that of a keyboard instrument . . .
. . . ma venghiamo a	But let us take
qualch'essempio particulare,	a particular example
per mostrare a quelli	to demonstrate to those
che vogliono nel Liuto i Semituoni	who want unequal semitones on the lute
disuguali, l'errore loro . . .	how they err . . .
vi mostrerò prima	First I shall show you
secondo la commune opinione	between which notes are found
tra quali corde si trouino	(according to common opinion)
i maggiori & i minori semituoni,	the major and minor semitones.
i quali vanno secondo	They go according to
l'ordine del sottoposto esēpio.	the pattern of the following example:[7]

8   Mag.   Mi.   Mag.   Mi.   Mag.   Mag.   Mi.   Mag.

The use of special frets, proposed earlier by Bermudo for pythagorean in-tonation, was suggested again by Jean Denis in the 1640s for meantone tem

7   Vincenzo Galilei 1584: 20.

perament. Denis was a harpsichord-maker. On one occasion when he encountered a man who had tuned a harpsichord in equal temperament, he told him that

il auoit mauuaise raison	it was poor thinking
de vouloir gaster le bon & parfait	to be willing to ruin a good and perfect
accord pour l'accomoder	tuning in order to accomodate it
a des Instruments imparfaits,	to imperfect instruments,
& qu'il falloit plustost chercher	and he should instead seek
la perfection du Luth & de la Viole,	to perfect the lute and the gamba,
& trouuer le moyen de faire que les	by finding a way to make its
semi-tons fussent majeurs & mineurs,	semitones major and minor
comme nous les auons sur l'Espinette,	as we have them on the harpsichord,
ce qui ne se peut faire auec les	which cannot be done with the
touches de cordes dont on touche les	tied-on frets with which one plays the
Luths, pource qu'il faudroit qu'elles	lute, because they would have
fussent faites en pieds de mousches;	to be staggered,
ce qui se peut faire par le moyen des	which can be done by means of
touches d'yuoire.	ivory frets.[8]

As far as I know, they were never adopted to any significant extent, certainly never enough to bring about any modification of the numbers or letters in tablature.

Even the fanatical Giovanni Battista Doni, who regarded equal temperament as 'a mere chimera and a non-existent, impossible thing',[9] acknowledged (around 1640) that temperament in general

è di due sorti, l'una	is of two sorts, the one
negl'instrumenti di manico;	in fretted instruments,
l'altra in quei di tasti:	the other in those with keys:
in quella le prime consonanze	in the former the primary consonances
sono più giuste,	[i.e. 5ths and 4ths] are more just,
e le seconde meno;	and the secondary ones [3rds and 6ths] less,
come anco i semituoni vi sono	and also the semitones therein are
alquanto piu diminuiti;	somewhat more diminished [sic];
ma in questa pel contrario	but in the latter, on the contrary,
più giuste si truovano	the 3rds and 6ths
le terze, e le seste,	are found [to be] more just,
e meno le quarte, e le quinte.	and the 4ths and 5ths less [so].
Il che è cagione, che i Liuti,	This is the reason that lutes,
le Tiorbe, le Viole, le Lire, &c.	theorbos, viols, liras [da braccio], etc.
mai perfettamente si possano accordare	can never be perfectly in tune
con i Clavicembali, e con l'Arpe	with harpsichords or with the harp,
per la diversità della participazione,	because of the difference in temperament,
come in un Discorso a parte	as (in another discourse)
è stato dottamente mostrato	has been learnedly demonstrated
del Bottrigari.	by Bottrigari.[10]

8   Denis 1650: 12.   9   Doni 1763a: 372.   10   Doni 1763a: 370.

Doni professed to regard it as astonishing that so many theorists had believed that fretted instruments had equal semitones,[11] and he advanced some remarkable arguments to the contrary:

Prendasi	Take
qualsiuoglia di questi instrumenti,	whichever of these instruments you wish,
sia Liuto, Chitarra, ò Viola,	be it a lute, guitar or viol,
poco importa; & si consideri vn poco,	it doesn't matter; and consider a bit
come vi stanno collocati i tasti;	how the frets are placed thereon;
& vedasi, se è vero, ch'il terzo	and see if it is true that the third
semituono sia maggiore	semitone is larger
di spatio materiale del secondo:	in actual space than the second;
et se è tale veramente in tutti	and if it is really so in all
gl'instrumenti, mi dichino vn poco,	the instruments, let them tell me a bit
come è possibile, che sia eguale	how it is possible that it should be equal
d'interuallo . . .	as a [musical] interval . . .[12]
Accordato, che hauerà vn Liuto, ò Viola,	Having tuned a lute or viol,
prenda vn'instrumento di 13. chorde,	take an instrument with thirteen strings
& di dodici semituoni eguali . . .	and twelve equal semitones [and compare] . . .
conoscerà manifestamente due cose:	two things will be manifestly known:
l'vna è, che quasi nessuna voce de' due	first, that almost no note on the two
instrumenti s'accorderà insieme,	instruments will be in tune together,
& vi sarà	and there will be
grandissima differenza d'accordo.	a very great difference in tuning;
L'altra, che in questo instrumento,	secondly, that in the instrument
geometricamente diuiso,	divided geometrically [for equal temperament],
nessuna consonanza quasi vi si trouerà:	almost no consonances will be found,
& riuscerà del tutto impraticabile.	and it will be wholly impracticable.[13]

About the time he wrote this, Doni was engaged in a dispute as to whether the organ in Bernini's new apse at S. Lorenzo in Damaso should be tuned in equal temperament, as Frescobaldi recommended.[14] So the description of equal temperament as 'impracticable' should not be taken as reflecting the full range of contemporary opinion. Indeed, if Doni had made these arguments in a debate his opponent might have replied that the first passage begs the question with an escape clause ('se è vero') and that the second makes no reference to expert players but merely asks the reader to compare his own tuning with equal temperament. It is appropriate to subject Doni's arguments to such meticulous scrutiny because he was in fact capable of being quite disingenuous. He would say of Frescobaldi, 'Il ne sçait pas ce que c'est semiton majeur ou mineur et ne joue guere sur les touches . . . chromatiques' ('He doesn't know what a major or minor semitone is, and hardly plays at all

11 Doni 1640: 285.   13 Doni 1640: 292.
12 Doni 1640: 286.   14 Doni 1647: 30-31.

on the chromatic keys').[15] He would argue that a player cannot produce euphonious intervals on an instrument fretted for equal semitones:

alcuno di questi, che non vorrebbono vedere nuoue perfettioni nella musica ... m'hà replicato, che con l'aiuto del dito si può supplire, quanto bisogna, à qualunque interuallo; ... questa è vna mera impostura: prima perché se bene nella Viola, ò Tiorba, per essempio, si possono con prolungare il dito oltre il tasto, inacutire le voci di qualche poco; tuttavia ciò à pena riesce in volerle abbassare. Secondo perche non è possibile far questa alteratione, se non in vna chorda sola. Terzo perche non si può fare d'vna misura certa, & determinata: anzi hora riuscirà più, hora meno ... Quarto perche non si possono fare queste alterationi in tempi veloci; & nelle note lunghe ancora non riesce di farle ne i primi loro incontri (perche l'vdito non puo giudicare di primo lancio, doue si richiedino), mà doppo, che l'orecchie hanno di già riceuuta la percossa, & l'offesa ...	One of those who do not wish to see new perfections in music replied to me that with the aid of the finger one can supply what is needed to any interval; ... [but] this is a mere imposture: first, because even if on the viol or theorbo (for example) one can by stretching the finger beyond the fret raise the notes some small amount, still that hardly will do in trying to lower them; secondly, because it is not possible to make this alteration, except on only one string [at a time]; thirdly, because it cannot be done by a specific and fixed amount – instead it will succeed now more, now less; fourthly, because one cannot make these alterations in fast tempos – and on long notes, indeed, one cannot make them at the outset of the note (because the ear cannot judge at the attack, when it is needed), but [only] after the ears have already received the attack and the offence.[16]

Any player will recognize that this is full of meretricious reasoning. Equally silly is the way Doni rejected Salinas' proof that lutes and viols were tuned in equal temperament. Salinas had said that on these instruments three major 3rds reached a full octave and therefore must have the lesser diesis (the amount by which three pure 3rds fall short of an octave) distributed among them. In reply, Doni cited the fact that these 3rds are larger than on a harpsichord as if this were contrary to Salinas' assertion rather than being its main point:

dice egli, nella Viola, ò Liuto tre ditoni, ò terze maggiori compiscono l'ottaua: dunque non vi sono le Diesi. Mà egli non s'accorge della fallacia: poiche allora sarebbe vera l'illatione, quando quei ditoni del Liuto, ò Viola fussero eguali à quei del Cembalo: il che si vede manifestamente essere falso; perche nella Viola, & Liuto sono molto maggiori, & più imperfetti, che nel Cembalo ...	He [Salinas] says that on a lute or viol, three ditones or major 3rds complete an octave; therefore there are no dieses. But he is not aware of his fallacy: since the inference would be true [only] if the ditones of the lute or viol were equal to those of the harpsichord, which is seen manifestly to be false because on the viol and lute they are much larger and more imperfect than on the harpsichord.[17]

15 Mersenne 1932-: VIII, 17.   17 Doni 1640: 289.
16 Doni 1640: 302-03.

It seems clear that Doni was capable of ludicrous arguments which he might have been dissuaded from publishing had he not held a position of bureaucratic eminence (as secretary to the College of Cardinals) or had fretted instruments not been, as a visitor to Rome wrote to Mersenne in 1634, 'quasi hors d'usage à Rome'.[18] If we were to assume that Doni never encountered a harpsichord in 1/6-comma meantone temperament (an assumption compatible with his statement that on keyboard instruments the 3rds were tempered less than the 5ths), then the 1/6-comma model would answer to his assertions that on the lute the 3rds were tempered more than on keyboard instruments, the 5ths were tempered less than the 3rds, and the distance from fret 2 to 3 was generally likely to be greater than from 1 to 2. But as the last assertion is uncorroborated elsewhere (so far as I know) I should hesitate to place very much weight upon it. Another descriptive remark by Doni about fretting strikes me as more feasible: he said that the exact location of fret 4 was likely to vary more than that of the others ('nel quarto poi si conosce maggiore variationi, che in tutti gl'altri').[19] Even in a fretting which would fall into the category of equal temperament in Table 1, there might be some leeway to mitigate the most salient defect of equal temperament – the rather impure 3rd between the middle courses – by inching fret 4 back as far as possible without compromising the purity of any unisons or octaves with fretted notes elsewhere on the instrument.

On balance, the evidence cited here confirms that even if some *players* achieved the more euphonious sound of a meantone temperament, *composers* after 1550 can hardly have expected it as they would on keyboard instruments. Thus the only period during which we might perhaps find the qualities and limitations of meantone forming part of the composer's implicit concept of his music for fretted instruments is the first half of the sixteenth century – after the plectrum, which had been inimical to solo polyphony, had fallen into disuse,[20] but before lutes and viols were codified as equal-temperament instruments. That was a period of notable refinement in lute design (see below, Appendix 4). It was also, as it happens, the period when books of music were first published, including music for lute and vihuela.

Are there instances where clues from the music itself may suggest meantone temperament? To answer this we must recall some of its technical characteristics. As in pythagorean intonation so in meantone temperament, the octave is made up of seven semitones of one size (the diatonic semitones) and five of another (the chromatic semitones). In pythagorean intonation the

---

18   Mersenne 1932–: IV, 5.
19   Doni 1640: 290-91.   20   See Poulton and Harwood 1980.

major 3rds are, as we have seen, a comma larger than pure, but since the diatonic semitones are smaller than the chromatic ones by virtually the same amount, the diminished 4th happens to form virtually a pure major 3rd. (A diminished 4th is, of course, made up of one chromatic and three diatonic semitones – for example E-F-F♯-G-A♭ – whereas a major 3rd contains two pairs of diatonic and chromatic semitones – for example E-F-F♯-G-G♯.) In any shade of meantone temperament, however, the diatonic semitones are distinctly larger than the chromatic ones, and the diminished 4th is therefore distinctly larger than a proper 3rd – enough, in fact, to be rather dissonant as a vertical sonority. Hence we should look for a composer who uses, let us say, the first fret for flats but avoids using it for G♯ in an E major triad, while favouring some other disposition of the same triad that is more difficult to play. We shall find such a composer in Luis Milán.

From Milán's naming of the *tono* or mode of each piece in his *El maestro* (1536)[21] it is clear that his music should be transcribed in terms of the A tuning (or rather, the A nomenclature for the open strings). Like other composers, Milán used the first fret for the diatonic semitone above the open string, as in Example 8, and often for the F major chord which appears at the end of the same example. But he avoided the E major triad a semitone lower, notwithstanding that it is even easier to play than the F chord and that he freely used the more awkward E chord at the end of Example 9 and the E-B-E sonority at the beginning of that example.

Example 8. Milán, Pavane 3 (1536), bars 11-16 (1927 edition: 136).

---

21 Schrade's is the most scrupulous modern edition (1927).

Example 9. Milán, Fantasia 14 (1536), opening (1927 edition: 68).

Occasionally he used the first fret for G♯, but – as Example 10 shows – always alone and cadencing to A: since the full chord is not played at once, a slight rubato can turn the harmonically out-of-tune G♯ to melodic advantage as a high leading-note. The dispensability, in this special context, of a proper harmonic intonation is confirmed in three of the last four cases in Example 10 (these four are from the second part of *El maestro*), where for the sake of facility the open G (alias F𝄪) stands in for F♯.[22]

Milán's music sounds better in meantone than in equal temperament. Not only is there more beating between about $1\frac{1}{2}$ and 6 times per second, which creates something of a warm *vox humana* effect, but also the sense of euphony is not disturbed, as it is in equal temperament, by a contrast between fast beating for the 3rds and 6ths and extremely slow for the 4ths and 5ths. That contrast becomes particularly evident when open-5th sonorities are mixed with triads, as in Examples 11 and 12. To my ear, Milán's music displays in meantone temperament a certain blend of poise and expressive opulence which equal temperament particularly disrupts at those moments.

Milán prefaced two pieces with an admonition to raise fret 4:

alçareys vn poco el quarto	raise a little the fourth
traste dela vihuela para que	fret of the vihuela so that
el punto del dicho traste	the note of the said fret
sea fuerte y no flaco . . .	be strong and not flaccid . . .
haueys de alçar el quarto	you have to raise the fourth
traste vn poco hazia las	fret a little towards the
clavijas dela vihuela . . .	keys of the vihuela . . .[23]

22   Hans Gerle as well used this device; see Dombois 1980: 66-67.
23   1927 edition: 68 & 358.

Example 10. Milán's use of fret 1 for G♯(1536). Bar numbers are indicated in each of the excerpts, which are from the following pieces (in order): Fantasias 4, 5 (twice), 6-9, 10 (twice), 11 and 13, the Romance *Sospirates baldovinos*, Fantasias 34 (twice) and 36, and the Soneto *Porta chiascun ne la fronte*.

Lutes, viols and temperaments

Example 11. Rate of beating, in various temperaments, for the harmonic intervals in the first two phrases of Milán's Fantasia 8 (1536; 1927 edition: 38), calculated at modern pitch for the G tuning, and discounting (for simplicity) the likelihood that some of the lower courses would be tuned in octaves.

equal temperament:

interval							
min. 3rd:		11			16	18	
maj. 3rd:		6		14	9	10½	14
4th:	1		1	1			1
5th:	½	½	½	½	1	1	½
maj. 6th:				12			12
maj. 10th:				7	5		7
12th:						½	

¼-comma meantone:

interval							
min. 3rd:		4			5½	6	
4th:	3		3	3½			3½
5th:	1½	1½	1½	1½	2	2½	1½
maj. 6th:				4			4
12th:					1		

⅕-comma meantone:

interval							
min. 3rd:		6			9	10	
maj. 3rd:		2		4½	3	3½	4½
4th:	2		2	3			3
5th:	1	1	1	1½	2	2	1½
maj. 6th:				6½			6½
maj. 10th:				2		1½	2
12th:					1		

⅙-comma meantone:

interval							
min. 3rd:		7			10	11	
maj. 3rd:		3		6	4	4½	6
4th:	2		2	2½			2½
5th:	1	1	1	1	1½	2	1
maj. 6th:				7½			7½
maj. 10th:				3		2	3
12th:					1		

Since the *clavijas* of a vihuela are its tuning pegs, this would actually lengthen the sounding portion of the string and lower the pitch. And since both pieces use the fret for D♯ and other notes a major 3rd above the open string (Examples 9 and 12 are from these pieces), 'fuerte y no flaco' evidently refers to the sonorous strength of the harmonic 3rd in some form of meantone, and not to the melodic strength of a high 3rd in pythagorean intonation. 'Flaco' describes quite well the effect in these examples when the first fret is at the wrong meantone position, whereas in pythagorean intonation the 'wrong' position would, as we have seen (cf. above, p. 12), give a particularly resonant 3rd. Enriquez de Valderrabano asked that for a piece in his *Silvas de sirenas* (1547) where the fret is used exclusively for E♭ (see Example 13

Example 12. Milán, *Con pavor recorda el moro* (1536), opening (1927 edition: 358).

Example 13. Valderrabano, 'Fantasia sobre vn Plenti [sic]' (1547), conclusion.

'the fourth fret be lowered a little toward the rose' ('baxer sea vn poco el quarto traste hazia el lazo'), and this confirms our interpretation of Milán's terminology.[24]

Milán did not always, however, avoid using fret 4 for *mi* and *fa* notes in the same piece. Often the B♮ can be treated like the G♯'s in Example 10. But once or twice in the first part of *El maestro*, and somewhat more often in the second part (which was for advanced players), E♭ and B♮ both appear pro-

---

24 Valderrabano 1547: 74ʳ. Ian Harwood has confirmed (to me) that renaissance lute terminology generally uses 'raise' in this sense and not to mean 'make the note sharper'.

minently in the same fantasia, as in Example 14.[25] Fret 6 as well is occasionally used for F and C♯ in the same piece.[26] An adroit player can handle these discrepancies *ad hoc* – that is, without equal temperament – but because of them the use of meantone temperament, though historically likely, will render certain passages more difficult to play. Table 5 summarizes Milán's use of the various frets.

Arnolt Schlick, the earliest composer to publish music for the lute, appears to have respected the limitations of meantone temperament more consistently. All but one of his fifteen extant lute pieces (1512) fit the following succession of semitones from the open string:[27]

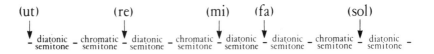

One piece, *Nach lust hab ich*, uses fret 1 for a chromatic semitone above the third course, but without using it on any other course at all (see Example 15). In 1511 Schlick published an exceptionally intricate and well-reasoned

Example 14. Milán, Fantasia 24 (1536), conclusion (1927 edition: 192).

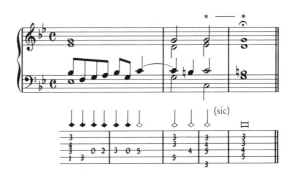

25 Analogous to the G♯'s in Example 10 are the B's at fret 4 in the following pieces: Romance 1, bars 28, 66 and 71 (1927 edition: 154 & 156); Fantasia 27, bar 45 (1927: 208); Fantasia 28, bar 124 (1927: 220); Fantasia 29, bar 26 (1927: 226); Fantasia 30, bars 123 and 201 (1927: 236 & 240); Fantasia 31, bar 103 (1927: 244).
26 Fret 6 is used in forty-seven pieces, never for any notes other than E♭, B♭, F, C♯ and A♭, but in ten pieces for both C♯ and one or more of the other notes. These are Fantasias 21, 24, 25, 26, 36, 37, 39 and 40, and Tentos 1 and 4. However, not all of them require that both the C♯ and the other note or notes be nicely in tune.
27 The lute pieces, which are to be found towards the end of Schlick 1512, are available in a good modern edition (1965).

Table 5. Implied names of the notes used by Luis Milán (1536) at each fingering position. The first column represents the open-string notes (at the nut); the second column represents those at fret 1; and so on. In equal temperament the frets would never require enharmonic adjusting or pairing, but in meantone they would for triadic concords.

open string	fret 1	fret 2	fret 3	fret 4	fret 5	fret 6	fret 7	fret 8	fret 9	fret 10
A	B♭	B	C	C♯D♭	D	E♭	E	F	F♯	G
E	F	F♯	G	G♯A♭	A	B♭	B	C	C♯	D
B	C	C♯	D	D♯E♭	E	F	F♯	G	G♯A♭	A
G	G♯A♭	A	B♭	B	C	C♯	D	E♭	E	F
D	E♭	E	F	F♯	G	A♭	A	B♭	B	C
A	B♭	B	C	C♯	D	E♭	E	F	F♯	G

Example 15. Schlick, *Nach lust hab ich* (1512), opening and a later excerpt. Schlick wrote the voice part in F major, and the lute part is here transcribed accordingly. In the middle of the second excerpt, the octave played at frets 1 and 4 would be sour in meantone temperament unless 1 were a *mi* fret like 4.

practical account of tempered tuning for the organ.[28] Clearly he had a sharp ear for intonation (perhaps on account of his blindness), and he might well have sought to accommodate his lute music to some form of meantone temperament. His organ tuning resembles 1/6-comma meantone but with an irregularity to allow the black note between G and A on the keyboard to serve as both A♭ (for an A♭ major triad) and G♯ (for a leading-note to A).[29] On a lute the irregularity would not be needed since the flat could be found at one point on the fingerboard and the sharp at another.[30]

In the meantone fretting implied by most of Schlick's music, the succession of major and minor semitones from the open string is exactly opposite to that of Oronce Fine's pythagorean fretting scheme (1530) and the mainstream of fifteenth-century theory for the chromatic monochord (see above, pp. 10-11). Such a perfect reversal might suggest why some authors of the late fifteenth and sixteenth centuries confused the theory of pythagorean ratios with the sound of meantone temperament.[31] If we suppose Fine to have been like them, we might take his pythagorean diagram as misrepresenting meantone in the same inadvertent way as did the pythagorean diagram published by Gafurio in 1518. This is speculative, of course, but Fine was the kind of theorist – in medieval terms a *musicus* and not a *cantor* – who might indeed run foul of the commonly acknowledged sixteenth-century cleavage between theoretical and practical music.[32]

Apart from Fine, the fretting schemes of two down-to-earth, 'unlearned' teachers, Hans Gerle (1532) and Silvestro Ganassi (1543), complement our musical evidence for the use of meantone temperament in the first half of the sixteenth century. Like all renaissance prescriptions except the 18:17 method, theirs put frets 5 and 7 at 1/4 and 1/3 of the distance from the nut to the bridge. But these rudimentary steps were so hoary with authority – and so easy to execute and then modify with a slight adjustment by ear – that they should be discounted if other parts of the fretting are contrary to pythagorean intonation.

Gerle put fret 1 at the location of a diatonic semitone above the open course in 1/6-comma meantone,[33] by a procedure rather more difficult to

28 Schlick 1511: ch. 8. Eitner's is a reliable modern edition (1869).
29 Husmann 1967: 253-56; Lindley 1974: 129-39.
30 For the analogous point in terms of pythagorean intonation, see the passage from Bermudo translated on pp. 17-18, above.
31 Lindley 1975-6: (see above, p. 11).
32 For example, Spataro (1521: 21ʳ) agreed with Ramis that 'in practice, that is, in musical usage and activity, the ditone corresponds to the 5:4 ratio, but not in speculative music . . . where the ditone corresponds to the ratio 81:64'.
33 In 1/6-comma meantone temperament, the 4th is 1/6 comma larger than pure, but the major 3rd is 1/3 comma larger, so the diatonic semitone (the difference between them) is 1/6 comma less than

carry out than the equivalent for equal temperament: he could have got the 17/18 position by putting the fret at 1/6 of the distance from the nut to fret 7 (since 1/6 of 1/3 is 1/18), but instead he put it at 2/11 of the distance, for a 31:33 position vis-à-vis the open string (2/11 of 1/3 being 2/33). He put fret 3 also at the position of a *fa* in 1/6-comma meantone (5/3 as far from fret 1 as that fret was from the nut).[34] He was vague about frets 4 and 8, saying merely that 4 should be 'between' 3 and 5, and that 8 should be closer to 7 than 7 was to 6. Eugen Dombois has examined and played Gerle's secular music of 1533 and concluded, notwithstanding a larger share of problems than I found in Luis Milán, that it is better served by 1/6-comma meantone than by equal temperament.[35] Here are Gerle's fretting instructions:

nym ein Richtscheytleyn das dinn sey	Take an [unmarked] straight-edge that is thin
oder sonst eyn ebens höltzlein	or else a flat piece of wood
gleych einem linial/vnd mach es	like a ruler, and make it
als lang/das es oben	of such a length that at the top it
anstee an dem höltzleyn da die	touches the piece of wood that the
saytten auflige[n] Unnd auch	strings lie on [i.e. the nut] and also
an stee an dem steg/da saytten	touches the bridge that the strings
aufligen vnd wann du	lie on, and when you
das richtscheytleyn hast gemacht/	have made the ruler
das es vnthen vnnd oben anstee/	so that it touches at both ends
nit das du es zu kurtz machst	(don't make it too short;
es muss anstee wie ich gesagt hab/	it must touch as I have said),
So zaychen das tail vnthen bey dem	mark the bottom part at the
steg mit einem.a. vnd das öbertayl	bridge with an *a*, and the top part
mit einem.b.damit du wissest	with a *b*, so that you will know
welchs ort zum steg gehört/Darnach	which end belongs to the bridge. Then
leg das richtscheitleyn auff ein	lay the ruler on a
disch vnd nym ein Circkel vnd such	table, and take a compass and find
das mittel an dem richtscheitleyn/	the middle of the ruler.
das merck mit einem punck oder	Mark it with a point or
düpflein vnd setz das.m.darzu/	little dot and put an *m* there.
Darnach tayl von dem.m.bis zu dem	Then divide from the *m* to the
.b.drey tayl/so	*b* [in] three parts; and

the difference between a pure 4th and 3rd. That just-intonation diatonic semitone has a frequency ratio of 16:15 (4:3 × 4:5); so we can calculate the number of cents in its 1/6-comma-meantone counterpart as follows: $(\log\frac{16}{15} - \frac{1}{6}\log\frac{81}{80}) \div \frac{\log 2}{1200} = 108.1$. The semitone from the nut to Gerle's fret 1 has a string-length ratio of 33:31; hence the number of cents is $\log\frac{33}{31} \div \frac{\log 2}{1200} = 108.2$.

34 Calculated as follows: Taking the open string length as 99 units, fret 7 is 33 units (1/3 of the total) down the neck; and fret 1 is 2/11 of 33, or 6 units down from the nut. Fret 3 is $1\frac{2}{3} \times 6$, that is, 10 units down from fret 1, for a total of 16 from the nut. Since 99 − 16 = 83, the string-length ratio for fret 3 is 99:83. Assuming uniform string thickness and density, and no change in tension when the string is pressed to the fret, this would give an interval of 305.2 cents $(\log\frac{99}{83} \div \frac{\log 2}{1200})$. The minor 3rd in 1/6-comma meantone temperament is a half-comma smaller than pure, so its calculation in cents is: $(\log\frac{6}{5} - \frac{1}{2}\log\frac{81}{80}) \div \frac{\log 2}{1200} = 304.9$.

35 Dombois 1980.

gibt dir der erst tayl von dem.m. | the first part from the *m* gives you
den sibenthen vnd vntersten griff | the seventh and lowest fret.
den merck mit einem dupff vnd setz | Mark it with a dot and put
die zyffer 7 darzu/darnach tayl | the number 7 there. Then divide
von der zyffer bis zu dem.b.aylff tayl | elevenfold from the number to the *b*,
vnd von der selben tayl zway | and two of the same parts
von dem.b.herab/geben dir den | down from the *b* give you the
ersten gryff den merck auch mit | first fret. Mark this also with
eynem tupff vnnd setz die zyffer.1. | a dot and put the number *1*
darzu/Darnach tayl wider von der | there. Then divide again from the
zyffer.7.bis zu dem.b.drey tayl vnnd | number 7 to the *b* threefold, and
der ein tayl von dem.b.herab | the first part down from the *b*
gibt dir den andern griff/den merck | gives you the second fret. Mark it
auch mit einem tupff vnd setz die | also with a dot and put the
zyffer.2.darzu/Darnach tayl von dem | number 2 there. Then divide from the
.m.bis zu dem.b.zwey tayl So | *m* to the *b* [in] two parts, and
gibt dir den ein tayl den fünfften | the one part gives you the fifth
griff den merck mit eynem dupff vnnd | fret. Mark it with a dot and
setz dir zyffer.5.darzu/ | put the number 5 there.
Darnach setz den sechsten gryff in | Then put the sixth fret in
die mit dess fünfften vnd sibenden | the middle of the fifth and seventh
gryffs den merck mit eynem dupff vnd | frets. Mark it with a dot and
setz die zyffer.6.darzu/Darnach tayl | put the number 6 there. Then divide
von der zyffer.1.bis zu dem.b.drei | from the number 1 to the *b* [in] three
tayl vnd wañ du die drey tayl hast/ | parts, and when you have the three parts
So gee mit vnuerrücktem circkel | then go with the compass unaltered
von der zyffer.1.herab noch fünff | down from the number 1 again five
geng das gibt dir den dritten gryff | spans; that gives you the third fret.
den merck mit eynem dupff vnnd setz | Mark it with a dot and put
die zyffer.3.darzu/ | the number 3 there.
Darnach setz den viertten gryff | Then put the fourth fret
zwischen den dritten vnnd fünfften | between the third and fifth
gryff/den merck mit eym dupff Und | frets. Mark it with a dot and
setz die zyffer.4.darzu . . . | put the number 4 there . . .
Wann aber eyner auff die lautten wolt | But if on the lute one wants
acht bundt machen/So mach er den | eight frets, then let him make the
achten bundt ein wenig enger von dem | eighth fret a little closer to the
sibenden bundt/wann der sechst steet. | seventh fret than the sixth is.[36]

Ganassi's rather longer discussion should be read with due allowance for his ubiquitous insistence that the player freely adjust the frets by ear:

voglio che questi duoi ricercari | I want these two ricercars
ti sia abastanza per quanto | to suffice for you for
lo ricercar l'istromento per | trying out the instrument for
il servitio, in parte di giustar | use, with respect to adjusting
li tasti & acordar le corde . . . | the frets and tuning the strings.[37]

---

36 Gerle 1532: preface. A facsimile of this paragraph is in Poulton 1972: 458; or see Pierce 1973: 143-48.
37 Ganassi 1543: Fi^r (ch. 16).

It is in chapter 4, entitled 'Regola di mettere li tasti', that the instructions themselves appear, starting with fret 2:

Nota bene che	Note well that
la proportione sesquiottaua si forma	the 9:8 proportion forms
il tono . . . alla prima parte	the whole-tone. At the first
delle ditte parte noue sera	of the said nine parts will be
il termine del . . . secondo tasto	the location of the second fret
ma scarso la grossezza del tasto	but minus the thickness of the fret,
e questo perche la natura	this being due to the nature
dello Strumēto . . .	of the instrument:
sonando la chorda uoda & puoi	after playing the open string,
. . . sonarla . . . con el dedo sul tasto	to play it with the finger on the fret
la se uien aforzao alquanto	makes it stretch somewhat.
. . . pero auertirai	But [in any case] remember
questo che habbiando messo li	that when you have placed the
tasti al modo che ti hauero mostrato	frets in the manner I shall show you,
. . . non mancar dil mouere il	do not [then] fail to move the
dito e ditti tasti piu e manco secōdo	said fret or frets up or down until
che laudito tuo si resta satisfatto.	your ear is satisfied.
. . . come . . . da l'Organo & da	As on the organ and
l'Istromēto di pena . . . e a uolere	harpsichord, it is desirable
. . . tenir alcūe qnte piu basse cioe	to keep some 5ths more low, i.e.
alquāto scarse de la sua uera	somewhat shy of their true
ītonatione altrimēti	intonation, otherwise
nō ci potria mai accordarlo . . .	you'll never be able to tune it.
io potrai qualque discorso de . . . la	I could discourse a bit on the
differētia del semitō maior al minor	difference between major and minor semitones,
& altre cose: ma . . . non acasca	etc., but it does not fall
in proposito in questa mia lettion	within the scope of my lesson
far tal ragionamento . . .	to give such an explanation.[38]

This passage implies a distinction between major and minor semitones, which would exclude equal temperament, and it identifies the viol's tempered 5ths with those heard on keyboard instruments, which were tuned in some form of meantone temperament. But to say that 'some 5ths' ('alcune quinte') were slightly smaller than pure suggests that some are not. This might conceivably refer to wolf 5ths here and there in the fretting scheme (D♯-B♭, G♯-E♭ and C♯-A♭). More likely it could be due either to some *ad hoc* irregularity in the tuning (Ganassi does say to adjust all the frets by ear) or else, perhaps, to the fact that in Ludovico Fogliani's imperfect account of meantone temperament (1529) the syntonic comma was distributed among the diatonic 5ths thus: F 0 C 0 G $\frac{1}{2}$ D $\frac{1}{2}$ A 0 E 0 B (and not F $\frac{1}{4}$ C $\frac{1}{4}$ G $\frac{1}{4}$ D $\frac{1}{4}$ A $\frac{1}{4}$ E $\frac{1}{4}$ B). No other theoretical model of meantone temperament – as opposed to practical descriptions for keyboard instruments – had yet been published.[39]

38 Ganassi 1543: Bii^r.   39 Lindley 198–: §2.

Certainly Ganassi himself could hardly have grasped the abstract nicety of distributing the comma evenly among a series of intervals. Even his informal 'tempering' of fret 2 is misrepresented in his diagram (Figure 11); and in his text he took an inordinate number of words merely to give the plain 3:4 position for fret 5:

Dapoi tu partirai la corda in	Then divide the string into
parte quatro, & la prima delle ditte	four parts, and the first of these
parte quattro sera il luoco del	four parts will be the location of the
quinto tasto elqual fa l'effetto	fifth fret, which produces the effect
della consonantia	of the consonant
quarta ouer diatesseron formasi della	4th or diatesseron, formed by the
proportione sesquitertia laqual e	4:3 proportion which is
intesa per questi dui numeri che e	derived from the two numbers
.4.a.3. pero partendo la corda	4 and 3; thus dividing the string
in parte quattro & puoi serarla al	into four parts and stopping it at the
termine della prima	location of the first
parte delle quattro et si uien a far	of the four parts, one achieves
il uero effetto della consonantia	the true effect of the consonant
quarta perche sonando la chorda uoda	4th, because playing the open string
e poi sonarlo o uoglia dire	and then playing it – or, rather,
pratticarla al termine della	using that portion which remains
quarta parte manco	with the fourth part set aside –
el uien a essere il contrasto delli	you will have the contrast between
dui numeri che e.4.a.3.	the two numbers which is 4:3.

Here are Ganassi's instructions, abridged, for frets 1, 3 and 4:

Dapoi che hauerai trouato &	Now when you have found and
terminato il ditto secōdo tasto	located the second fret
cō il modo ditto di sopra	by the method given above,

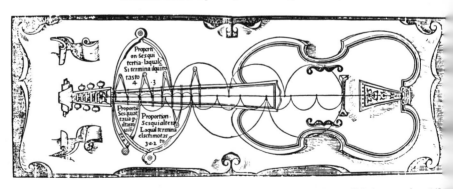

Figure 11. Ganassi's illustration of fret locations (1543: ch. 4). Fret 2 is shown slightly more than 1/9 of the distance from the nut to the bridge. This is mistaken: it is contrary to Ganassi's instructions, which say it should be slightly less; it makes the ratio of string lengths greater than 9:8, whereas in all the traditional regular schemes of temperament, including equal temperament, it is smaller; and in practice it would aggravate the enlargement of the whole-tone which is due to the fact that the string's tension is increased when it is pressed to the fret.

il tasto primo sera terminato al mezo	the first fret is located halfway
tra il scagneleto del manico al	between the nut and the
secondo tasto ma de piu zoe	second fret, but more, i.e.
battēdo di fora la mita della	down the neck by half the
grosseza del tasto . . . & in questo	fret's width. In this regard
ti haueria possuto resonar il	I could have calculated[40] for you the
partimento del semiton maior al minor	division of major and minor semitones.
. . . il primo tasto elqual fa leffeto	The first fret gives the effect
del semiton minor . . . torai quella	of the minor semitone. Take the
medēma distātia che e dal primo	same distance as from the first
al secondo & hauerai trouato	to the second fret and you will have
il termine . . . del . . . terzo tasto . . .	the location of the third fret.
Et il quarto tasto sera al uero mezzo	And the fourth fret will be midway
fra il terzo e quinto tasto.	between the third and fifth frets.

Notice the apparent contradiction between adjusting fret 1 down the neck (which will raise the pitch) and saying that it makes, in effect, a minor semitone. What should we make of this? In Ganassi's tuning checks (see Example 1) and in the two ricercars referred to in the passage translated above on p. 60, fret 1 is employed several times for *fa* notes but never for a *mi*.[41] So we have three possibilities. (1) He wanted pythagorean intonation, in which *fa* would indeed make a minor semtition – that is, a limma – from the open-string note. This interpretation would be quite difficult to

---

40   I am grateful to Mirko Caffagni for correcting my translation here: I had mistakenly seen resonance rather than reason in 'resonar'.

41   When fret 1 is *fa*, the open string will be *mi* and the note immediately above *fa* in the diatonic scale will be at fret 3, as in the last three bars of the first ricercar:

Ganassi's only exception to this use of fret 1 is in an illustration of diminutions (right after ch. 21), where the C♯ is so fleeting that its high intonation would not be minded, I think (indeed, the contrast with C♮ would be more telling):

reconcile with Ganassi's explicit reference to tempered 5ths. (2) He wanted equal temperament, and 'minor semitones' meant 18:17. This would go well with the fact that fret 1 is shifted up from a 9:8 position, but it would be awkward to reconcile with Ganassi's almost exclusive preference for *fa* notes at fret 1 and with his references to major as well as minor semitones and to tempering the 5ths as on the organ and harpsichord. Not impossible, however. (3) He wanted some form of meantone temperament, and in his use of the term 'minor semitone' he was, like so many early-sixteenth-century theorists, confusing the theoretical model of pythagorean intonation with the reality of meantone tuning. This choice is perhaps easiest to reconcile with the other evidence in the text.

There remain frets 6, 7 and 8:

Dapoi partirai la corda in parte tre	Then divide the string in three parts,
& la prima de esse tre parte sera	and the first of these three will be
il termine del settimo tasto . . .	the location of the seventh fret.
Dapoi il sexto tasto sera terminato	Then the sixth fret will be located
al mezzo del spacio fra il quinto e	midway between the fifth and
settimo ma scarso cioe tenirlo	seventh, but less, i.e. put it
de dentro il compasso la grossezza del	up the neck by the width of the
tasto & la sera il suo termine.	fret and *there* will be its location.
Et l'ottauo tasto per il suo termine	And the location of the eighth fret
sera quella medēma portion che e dal	will be the same portion as from the
quinto al sexto . . .	fifth to the sixth [sic].

If we disregarded Ganassi's instructions to shift frets 2 and 6 towards the nut by the fret's own width, and to shift fret 1 towards the bridge by half that amount, and if we ignored his advice to adjust every fret by ear, we could naively infer the following chain of ratios from the nut to fret 3: 18:17:16:15, and then from fret 3 to 8 the chain 20:19:18:17:16:15. But Ganassi did not want this. Towards the end of chapter 4 he rejected a 5:6 position for fret 3:[42]

la ₚportione sesquitertia . . . & . . .	The 4:3 and
sesquialtera . . . questi e	3:2 proportions: these are
la proportione principale in questo	the principal proportions in this
mio modo . . . ti haueria potuto dire	method of mine. I could have told you
che la proportione sesquiquinta	that the 6:5 proportion
haueria trouato il termine del terzo	would give the location of the third
tasto . . . dapoi ancora si haueria	fret, and again one might
possuto regolar il termine del quarto	have set the location of the fourth
tasto con la proportione sesquiquarta	fret with the 5:4 proportion,
. . . ma . . . la natura & altro del-	but the nature etc. of the
l'istrumento mi moue . . . piu del	instrument prompts me rather to the
modo che ti ho regolado . . .	method which I have given you.

---

42 Of course 5:6 is the same as 15:18 and would result from Ganassi's geometry without his qualifications.

And later, in the chapter on tuning the open strings, he reiterated the admonition to adjust the frets by ear, and at the same time gave a further hint of meantone temperament by suggesting that one should be particularly concerned about the sound of double stops and of chords in ensemble music, but without expecting purity in the 5ths:

Nota che quando hauerai agiustado	Note that if you have adjusted
li tasti & acordado le corde	the frets and tuned the strings
con il modo disopraditto & che ancora	by the method given above and still
non te riuscisse tal accordo . . .	have not arrived at a tuning
in quella perfettiõ che fusse	as perfect as might be
desiderata dal tuo bono audito come	desired by your good ear, for instance
sonando il tuo Stromento a consonantie	when playing multiple stops
ancora in cõpagnia d'altri stromenti	or in ensemble music,
questo si potra acadere per il mancar	this could be due to a lack
della diligentia del'audito tuo &	of diligence in your ear,
ancora rispetto il natural della	and also [might] involve the nature of the
musica in quanto l'effetto suo che e	musical effect, i.e.
quelle quinte scarse gia ricordate	those tempered 5ths already mentioned;
per inanti per tanto	but in any case
tutte accomoderai con il	you will accommodate them all by
mouere il tasto piu e mãco tanto che	moving the fret up or down until
non si uenga adispiaciere alla orecchia . . .	the ear is no longer displeased.[43]

Ganassi was neither ahead of his time as a theorist of temperaments nor very concerned with exact regularity in his tuning. But to the extent that his musicianship would require a modicum of regularity (see p. 8 above), his instructions answer to meantone better than to any other theoretical model.

None of the evidence for meantone temperament before 1550 is perfectly incontrovertible, yet the total quite justifies its use by players today who are adept enough to carry it off and whose ear tells them that the music is particularly well served. There are two ways to tune it: by tempering the open strings first, and adjusting the frets to match, or else by placing the frets first, and tuning the open strings to match.

The first method requires a sharp ear for beats. To avoid the extreme of 1/4-comma meantone, let the open 3rd beat about once per second and make the 4ths and the two available major 6ths (on the viol the latter must be plucked, of course) beat according to their pitch (whatever it may be in the case of any given pair of strings) in keeping with the following approximate guidelines (calculated in terms of modern pitch, a' = 440):

43 Ganassi 1543: ch. 6, last paragraph.

If the open 12ths sound too flat, make subtle adjustments, even at the expense of opening out the major 3rd very slightly and letting the 6ths beat once more per second. When the open strings have been tempered, adjust the frets for perfect unisons and octaves and for 5ths that are noticeably tempered but not sour.

Instruments with a low action (so that there is little change of string tension when a fret is used) are best for the second method, which Eugen Dombois published with tables for 1/4-comma meantone and two varieties approximating to 1/6-comma.[44] Table 6 gives equivalent data in simpler form for frets 1 to 9 in 1/4- and 1/5-comma meantone. On an instrument marked out with the positions for both varieties, one may readily compare them, or put all the frets at a compromise position for 2/9-comma meantone temperament.

Table 6. Fret positions for 1/4- and 1/5-comma meantone temperament.

fret		% of string length down from the nut for	
		1/4-comma meantone	1/5-comma meantone
1 {	*mi*	4.3	4.7
	fa	6.54	6.25
2		10.56	10.67
3		16.4	16.25
4 {	*mi*	20.0	20.2
	*fa*****	21.88	21.5
5		25.23	25.2
6 {	*mi*	28.45	28.7
	fa	30.12	29.86
7		33.13	33.17
8		37.5	37.34
9		40.2	40.3

*If fret 4 is set for *fa*, the unison method naturally cannot be used for tuning the middle pair of courses.

44 Dombois 1974: 84 & 88. A more precise value for fret 1 as *mi* in 1/4-comma meantone temperament would be 4.2977%.

5 Just intonation

A weighty tome could be filled with theories ill founded upon a faith in simple ratios. For the purposes of this little book, however, an ounce of just-intonation schemes critically examined will be worth a pound of such schemes enthusiastically entertained. According to *The new Grove* the very concept of 'Just [pure] intonation' is an elusive one whose meaning depends upon circumstance:

> When pitch can be intoned with a modicum of flexibility, the term 'just intonation' refers to the consistent use of harmonic intervals tuned so pure that they do not beat, and of melodic intervals derived from such an arrangement, including more than one size of whole tone . . . On normal keyboard instruments, however, the term refers to a system of tuning in which some 5ths (often including D-A or else G-D) are left distastefully smaller than pure in order that the other 5ths and most of the 3rds will not beat.

Grove does not say how the term is to be applied to fretted instruments. Do they have a 'modicum of flexibility'? In reality it all depends upon the player. On normally fretted instruments, untempered intervals entail skilful fudging. For some music the extent of the fudging could be minimized by tuning the open strings to some shade of meantone temperament and fretting the instrument accordingly, but even without that advantage, good viol consorts often manage, after warming up, to produce justly intoned chords at cadences and at other moments when the musical texture is relatively simple. On the lute it is more difficult, for several reasons: the sound fades; the player has more notes to deal with; the action is lower; the pressure can be varied only by the left hand and not the right.

Just-intonation fretting schemes are produced by theorists who make no allowance for such fudging. The instrument itself is to render each note either pure or else out of tune by an entire comma or even a diesis (rather much for the player to fudge, particularly among the first few frets). We have seen that in pythagorean intonation the major 3rd between the middle courses is a comma larger than pure. In just intonation it will be pure, but then one of the 4ths among the other courses must be a comma larger than

67

pure if the interval between the outer courses is not to fall shy of two octaves by that amount.

For a clear understanding of just-intonation fretting proposals, it is well to be mindful of their various distinctive purposes, and of whether they are for the ordinary number of normal frets or require special equipment. Doni's *violetta diaharmonica*,[1] for example, was one of several instruments by which he hoped to revive the ancient Greek modes (Figure 12), whereas Thomas Perronet Thompson's enharmonic guitar (1829) was for his daughter's instruction and amusement (Figure 13).

On the viol which Thomas Salmon demonstrated to the Royal Society in 1705,[2] 'the frets for the several strings do not stand in a straight line', according to his own description, 'and the places are also shifted in different keys', except that in the case of each major key and its relative minor 'one finger-board will be sufficient for both'. For C major and A minor the frets were arranged ('with a particular fret for each string') so that 16:15 was always the ratio for E-F and B-C, 10:9 for D-E and G-A, and 9:8 for C-D, F-G and A-B. Each whole-tone was then divided arithmetically – 20:19:18 for the small ones and 18:17:16 for the large (see Figure 14). Salmon declared that with these semitones the ear had a 'satisfactory pleasure which arises from the exactness of sonorous numbers'. He did not explain how it would suit the ear, in C major or A minor, to have D-A a comma smaller than pure and to have A-C♯ and B♭-D larger than pythagorean.[3] 'The proportions offered were the same', he said, 'that the ancient Grecians used . . . and the practical musican will testify that these are the best notes he ever heard.'[4]

Very early in the seventeenth century Andreas Reinhard in Schneeberg had derived exactly the same scale, allegedly 'from the good old authors, and especially Vitruvius and Macrobius',[5] and found that it helped to explain the symmetry of the universe (see Figure 15). As J. Murray Barbour has noted, Reinhard's friend Abraham Bartolus (1614) 'advocated the same method for keyboard instruments, and later prescribed it also for fretted instruments and

1 Doni 1763a: 376-96.
2 See Tilmouth 1980 for a nice account of Salmon's uproarious career in music.
3 In Salmon's 1705 scheme for C major and A minor, the 5th D-A was a comma smaller than pure, with a ratio of 40:27 instead of 3:2, and a decrease in string length of $32\frac{1}{2}$% instead of $33\frac{1}{3}$%. The 3rds A-C♯ and B♭-D had ratios, respectively, of 108:85 and 51:40, and decreases in string length of 21.3% and 21.6% instead of 20% as in a pure 3rd.
4 Salmon 1705: 2069 (sic).
5 Bartolus 1614: 107. Actually Vitruvius was in musical matters an undiluted Aristoxenian who never mentioned monochord ratios and treated musical intervals as discrete quantities of vocal pitch (*c*1486 edition: book V, ch. 4). Regarding Macrobius, see p. 30 above.

69

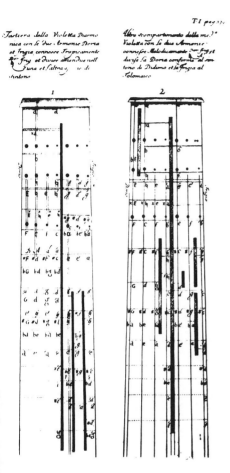

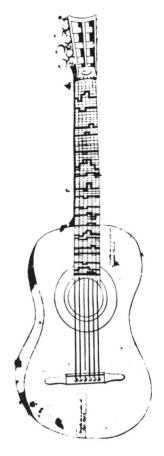

Figure 12. Doni's fretting arrangements for the viola da gamba to play the ancient Greek modes (1763a: 379).

Figure 13. Thompson's design for a just-intonation guitar (1829: frontispiece).

$$\text{Tone Major }\tfrac{8}{9} \quad \text{Tone Minor }\tfrac{9}{10} \quad \text{Hemitone }\tfrac{15}{16} \quad \text{Tone Major }\tfrac{8}{9} \quad \text{Tone Minor }\tfrac{9}{10} \quad \text{Tone Major }\tfrac{8}{9} \quad \text{Hemitone }\tfrac{15}{16}$$

An Octave with a greater Third. $C \tfrac{17}{18} C \tfrac{16}{17} D \tfrac{19}{20} D \tfrac{18}{19} E \tfrac{15}{16} F \tfrac{17}{18} F \tfrac{16}{17} g \tfrac{19}{20} g \tfrac{18}{19} a \tfrac{17}{18} a \tfrac{16}{17} b \tfrac{15}{16} c.$

$A \tfrac{17}{18} A \tfrac{16}{17} B \tfrac{15}{16} C \tfrac{17}{18} C \tfrac{16}{17} D \tfrac{19}{20} D \tfrac{18}{19} E \tfrac{15}{16} F \tfrac{17}{18} F \tfrac{16}{17} g \tfrac{19}{20} g \tfrac{18}{19} a.$ An Octave with a lesser Third

Figure 14. Salmon's scale for C major and A minor (1705: 2041 (sic)).

70   *Lutes, viols and temperaments*

bells'.[6] Bartolus said that on the organ Reinhard's scheme eliminated the wolf,[7] which of course is rubbish. Just how familiar Bartolus was with fretted instruments may be seen from his diagrams employing lute tablature, according to which *a* (in French tablature) and *0* (in Italian tablature) refer to frets 1, 4 and 6; *e* and *4* refer to fret 3; and so on (Figure 16).

Mersenne's just intonation (1637) wants perhaps a gentler debunking, as he hardly meant it himself. For keyboard instruments, yes: he illustrated five special designs and discussed their merits after explaining why just intonation is infeasible on normal instruments (one reason was that 'D cannot have

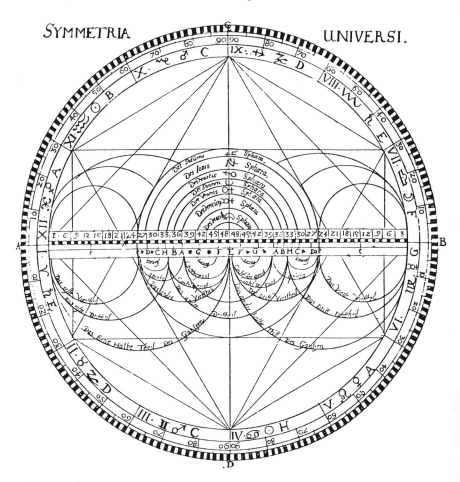

Figure 15. Cosmic implications of Reinhard's just-intonation monochord (Bartolus, 1614).

6 Barbour 1951: 101; Bartolus 1614: 165.
7 Bartolus 1627: 126. For more on Bartolus see Damann 1969.

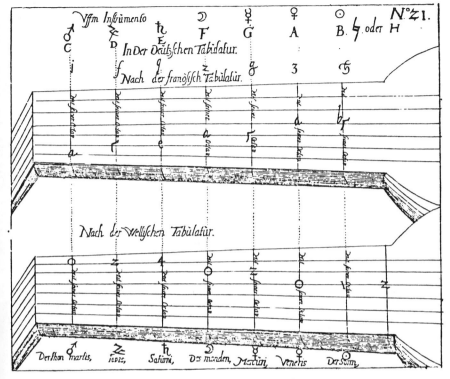

Figure 16. Bartolus' concept of French and Italian tablature (1614: 172).

a pure 4th below, since it has a pure 5th [sic] above').[8] One of these designs which he particularly advocated[9] was actually used by Joan Albert Ban in the 1640s (Figure 17). Mersenne also discussed equal temperament for keyboard instruments, in addition to giving step-by-step instructions for 1/4-comma meantone ('la manière d'accorder parfaictment les Orgues or-dinaires'). It is fair to say that Mersenne paid a great deal of attention to the subject of tuning and temperament.[10] So it is remarkable that in spite of his friendship and faithful correspondence with Doni[11] he managed to avoid pro-

8   Mersenne 1636-7: III, 351 ('Le D ne peut auoir la Quarte iuste en bas, lors qu'il a la Quinte iuste en haut'). The nearest diagram depicts A as a wolf 5th to D.
9   Mersenne 1636-7: III, 351-54 ('although the nineteen keys of its octave may be, it seems, more dif-ficult to play than the thirteen of other keyboards, nevertheless the perfection of . . . this . . . key-board abundantly repays the difficulty of playing, which organists will be able to surmount in the space of one week . . . one need not feel pity for the pains, nor evade the work, which leads to per-fection' etc.).
10   Lindley 1980b.
11   Letters from Doni to Mersenne before 1637, most of which discuss tuning, have been published in the *Correspondance du P. Mersenne* (1932-): I, 437; II, 30; III, 506 & 531; IV, 86 & 304; V, 32, 386, 409, 522 & 524; VI, 17 & 70.

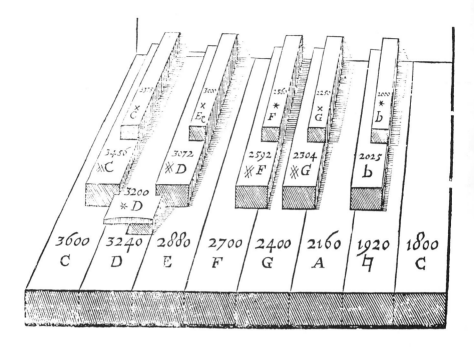

Figure 17. Ban's just-intonation keyboard design (1643: 28).

posing that players adopt or even experiment with any one form of just intonation on fretted instruments. A quick glance at his *Harmonie universelle* cannot show this, but a systematic review of the pertinent sections will reveal that as far as fretted instruments were concerned Mersenne regarded just intonation as so much theoretical baggage and not a practical issue.

In volume III, which amounts to an encyclopaedia of all the musical instruments known to Mersenne, the first four books discuss string instruments. Book I is introductory and covers general monochord theory. Book II is about plucked fretted instruments: book III deals with the spinet, clavichord, harp and so on; book IV is about bowed instruments.

Book II starts with the lute, and Proposition I includes a preliminary discussion of its fretting, by way of explaining the four columns of numbers in Figure 18. On a C string the first three columns would give the following configurations of pitch classes (here I represent the various pure intervals as follows: 5ths or 4ths: ⬡ ; major 3rds or minor 6ths: ⬠ ; minor 3rds or major 6ths: ⬡):

first column[12]

second column[13]

third column

(Figure 17 matches the second set.) When applied to six courses tuned by pure 4ths and a pure major 3rd, each fretting would produce an elaborate set of pitch classes amongst which the player would have to choose carefully to avoid the many sour unisons, octaves, 5ths, etc. Assuming the courses were named A-D-G-B-E-A (as the notation in the upper left corner of Figure 18 implies), the following configurations would be generated:[14]

first column[15]

second column

third column

Mersenne neglected to propose that lutenists use any of these frettings in particular. We can form some idea of what such a proposal might entail by looking at Dyrck Rembrantz van Nierop's account, published in 1659, of a

12 It would have been more logical for G♯ to make pure 3rds with E and B ( ) than a pure 5th with C♯.

13 In this arrangement each diatonic note is provided with every possible triadic concord (if we take the two D's a comma apart as representing one note).

14 To grasp the logic of these configurations, imagine an instrument with only one fret, say 1/5 of the distance from the nut to the bridge. In that case any open string ('x') would have its pure major 3rd: , and the diagram of pitch classes available on one or another of the six courses would be obtained as follows:

15 Pitch classes in the relation are for all practical purposes identical (as discussed on p. 12 above, with reference to pythagorean intonation), and therefore in this scheme the F in the lower left corner (which is produced by fret 10 on the G course) will make a good octave with the E♯ at the far right (produced by fret 8 on the bass course); and the G to the far left (produced by fret 10 on the other A course) will make a good octave with F♯(produced by fret 8 on the B course).

74

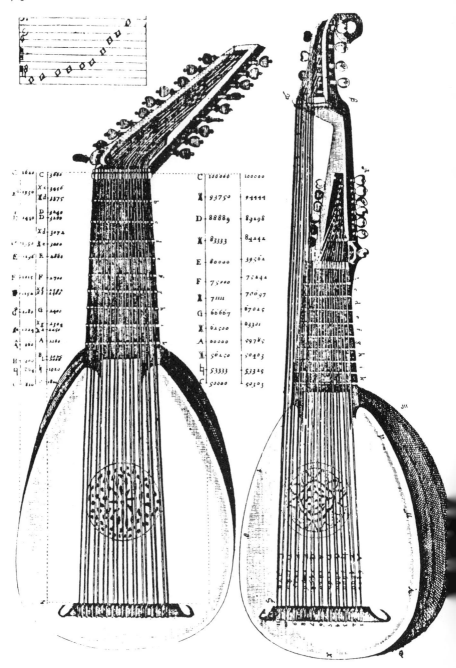

Figure 18. Mersenne's just-intonation fretting calculations for the lute (1636-7: 46). (Four numbers were mistranscribed in the engraving: 89298 should be 89198, and 75242 should be 75142; 39562 should be 79562, and 70697 should be 70967.)

just-intonation cittern (see Figure 19).[16] Van Nierop showed that if the four courses of this relatively simple instrument were tuned as follows:

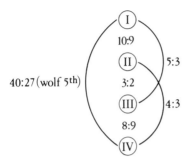

then with his proposed fretting, each position on the highest course could be supplied with one or more justly intoned chords as shown in Example 16. The fourth column in Figure 18, with fret 12 at 50.36% of the distance from the bridge to the nut, represents a succession of twelve 17:18 semitones.[17]

Example 16. Van Nierop's list of serviceable chords on his justly intoned cittern (see Figure 19). Courses I and IV are tuned to form a wolf 5th. (Fret 4 makes a whole-tone above fret 3: this is normal for a cittern.)

16 Van Nierop 1659: 44. For more on van Nierop, see Barbour 1934 and Lindley 198-: §5. About the cittern, Mersenne said that 'plusieures maistres' made use of a just-intonation method (1636-7: III, 98ʳ), but he also said (97ᵛ):

> Quant a la distance des touches,   As for the distance of the frets,
> les Facteurs la determinent par   makers determine it by
> oreille, comme celle des autres   ear, as on the other
> instrumens a touches, car ils   fretted instruments, for they
> les haussent & les baissent   raise and lower them
> iusques a ce que les accords   until the intervals
> leur satisfacent . . .   satisfy them.

17 Since each fret is 1/18, or 5.5%, down the neck from the next higher fret (for a string length of 94.4%), the values can be checked on a pocket calculator by multiplying 0.9̄4̄ in succession until 0.50364 is reached for fret 12.

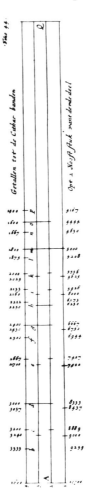

Figure 19. Van Nierop's fretting scheme for a justly intoned cittern (1659: 44).

Here is Mersenne's discussion of these four systems:

<table>
<tr>
<td>

Or l'on appelle *Temperament*,
l'alteration que l'on fait des
interualles tant consonãs que
dissonãs, dont i'ay expliqué
les vrayes raisons, & les iustes
proportiõs dans les liures de
la Theorie, & mesme dans cette
proposition, lors que i'ay
expliqué l'accord du

</td>
<td>

'Temperament' is the name of
the alteration that one makes to the
intervals (consonant as well as
dissonant) – of which I have explained
the true [untempered] ratios and just
proportions in the books on
theory and likewise in this
proposition, where I have
explained the tuning of the

</td>
</tr>
</table>

Tuorbe, [open strings of the] archlute[18]
comme s'il eust esté iuste, as if it were just
& en sa perfection. and in its perfection.
Ce temperament This temperament [i.e. not just
est marqué à costé du intonation] is marked next to the
Tuorbe, & cõsiste en 12 archlute, and consists of twelve
demitons égaux, esquels [sic] equal semitones into which
l'Octaue est divisée, & se trouue the octave is divided, and is found
en diuisant les chordes à vuide, by dividing the open strings
ou le Luth depuis (or [the distance on] the lute from
le fillet iusques au cheualet the nut to the bridge)
en 100000 parties, dont le *b* into 100,000 parts, of which *b*
c'est à dire la premiere touche (that is, the first fret)
en a 94444 . . . has 94,444 . . . [here the other numbers are listed]
50363, represente la moitié de la 50,363 represents half of the
chorde, encore que ce nombre soit string, yet this number is
trop grãd de 363. puisque 50000 too large by 363, since 50,000
est sousdouble de 100000. C'est is half of 100,000. That is
pourquoy i'ay mis l'autre rang des why I have given the other row of
nombres, qui donne les numbers, which gives
demi-tons beaucoup plus iustes much more just semitones
que le premier, comme l'on void en than the first, as one sees by
comparant les vns aux autres. comparing them.
Mais les deux autres rangs des But the other two rows of
nombres qui sont à costé gauche numbers that are at the left side
du Luth mõstrent la distance des of the lute show the spacing of the
touches dans leur plus grande frets in their greatest
perfection, dont le premier a perfection: the first row has
seulement 13 nombres pour marquer only thirteen numbers to mark
les 12 demitons qui font l'Octaue the twelve semitones that make the octave
du Luth: & le second rang monstre on the lute; and the second row shows
qu'il faut 19 touches . . . pour les that nineteen frets are needed for the
trois Genres . . . , comme i'ay three genera [of Greek music], as I
dit dans les liures de la Theorie, said in the books on theory,
dont on peut tirer d'autres manieres from which one can derive other ways
pour diuiser le manche du Luth. of dividing the lute's fingerboard.
Plusieurs Facteurs d'instrumens Many instrument makers
diuisent la longeur du Luth, ou de divide the length of the lute (or of
la chorde à vuide en 18 parties, dont the string) into eighteen parts of which
la 17 fait la premiere touche; & puis the seventeenth makes the first fret, and then
ils diuisent le reste de la chorde they divide the rest of the string
en 18 parties, dont ils en prennent into eighteen parts, of which they take
encor 17 pour faire le second again seventeen to make the second
demiton, & ainsi consequemment iusques semitone, continuing thus until
a ce qu'ils ayent 8. ou 9. demi-tons. they have eight or nine semitones.[19]

Having thus explained how one goes about the 17:18 method, Mersenne

---

18 As Spencer points out (1976: 416), 'In the text Mersenne called this instrument *Tuorbe*, but in his errata he wrote that the Italians called it *Arciliuto* though he would have preferred *Luth à double manche*.'
19 Mersenne 1636-7: III, 48.

then gave in Proposition III (Proposition II being about other matters) an equivalent step-by-step method for yet another scheme of just intonation, with alternative positions (9:10 as well as 8:9) for fret 2. The pitch classes involved would be:

on a C course[20]

applied to six courses (A-D-G-B-E-A)

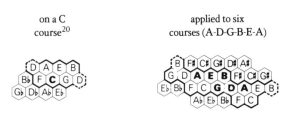

Mersenne's comments on fret 2 show that neither the 8:9 nor the 9:10 position was actually used or intended for use; and his reversal of the two (he said that for a major tone the first fret should be higher than for a minor one) suggests that he himself never tried them out:

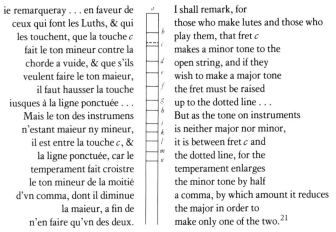

ie remarqueray . . . en faveur de ceux qui font les Luths, & qui les touchent, que la touche c fait le ton mineur contre la chorde a vuide, & que s'ils veulent faire le ton maieur, il faut hausser la touche iusques à la ligne ponctuée . . . Mais le ton des instrumens n'estant maieur ny mineur, il est entre la touche c, & la ligne ponctuée, car le temperament fait croistre le ton mineur de la moitié d'vn comma, dont il diminue la maieur, a fin de n'en faire qu'vn des deux.	I shall remark, for those who make lutes and those who play them, that fret c makes a minor tone to the open string, and if they wish to make a major tone the fret must be raised up to the dotted line . . . But as the tone on instruments is neither major nor minor, it is between fret c and the dotted line, for the temperament enlarges the minor tone by half a comma, by which amount it reduces the major in order to make only one of the two.[21]

The last sentence would be true only of 1/4-comma meantone temperament, but this was just an abstract confusion and not a proposal for meantone temperament on the lute. Mersenne generally took it quite for granted that the lute was played in equal temperament, which he discussed thoroughly in Propositions V to VII (after reviewing Ptolemy's summary of ancient Greek intervallic theory in Proposition IV and the first part of V). He delighted in

20   This can be derived from the 18-note scheme on p. 73 above by favouring those 'chromatic' frets which produce notes lying in the upper half of the whole-tone (as frettings for meantone temperament tend to do, but not those for pythagorean intonation).

21   Mersenne 1636-7: III, 55. Mersenne's use of the term 'instrumens' here reminds one that the German cognate sometimes meant 'keyboard instruments'.

Figure 20. Mersenne's just-intonation values for the open-string pitches of the gamba (1636-7: 192).
The ratios would be expressed more simply if the numbers were divided by 4 (20:27:36:45:60:80).

presenting myriad ways to find equal-temperament positions for the frets, and he habitually referred to fretted instruments as being in equal tempera- ment. He would remark, 'This does not impede one in the slightest from using equal tones and semitones on the lute',[22] or 'All makers of these in- struments are disciples of Aristoxenus';[23] or, in regard to the viol in book IV:

la diuision du manche de la Viole . . .	The division of the viol's fingerboard
n'est pas differente de celle du	is not different from that of
manche du Luth; c'est pourquoy	the lute's fingerboard. That is why
i'adiouste seulement icy une	I add here only one
nouuelle maniere pour le diuiser,	new way to divide it,
dont i'ay donné l'inuention dans	the invention of which I have given in
la quatorze & quinzieme Proposition	Propositions XIV and XV
du premier liure, & dans la septieme	of book I, and in Proposition VII
du second liure.	of book II.[24]

Various statements in this vein show that for lutes and viols Mersenne re- garded just intonation as a theoretical phenomenon and not a viable practice. It is true that he gave just-intonation numbers for the open courses. In Figure 20 the D's at 320 and 80 are a comma out with the A at 108 (since 1/3 of 320 is $106\frac{2}{3}$): here he overlooked the need for the intervals among the open strings to match those of the fretting scheme. This defect was evaded in the set of numbers near the bridge of the archlute in Figure 18, where the two A's are duly a comma out with each other at 1620 and 6400; but in this instance Mersenne implied that the numbers were fictitious by saying that they represented the archlute's tuning *as if* it were just (the passage is trans- lated on p. 77 above), and indeed anyone who tried to use them would have found that they were all upside down, with the longest monochord portion for the highest note.[25]

22 Mersenne 1636-7: III, 61 ('Ce qui n'empesche nullement que l'on n'vse de l'esgalité des tons, et des demy-tons sur le Luth').
23 Mersenne 1636-7: III, 60 ('tous les Facteurs de ces instruments sont disciples d'Aristoxene').
24 Mersenne 1636-7: III, 199.
25 If he meant to suggest frequency ratios and not monochord ratios, this would confirm that he was dealing in theory rather than practice, as there was yet no accurate way to measure frequencies.

6 Other schemes

In his son Robert's *Varietie of lute lessons* (1610) John Dowland published a set of fretting instructions after those of Hans Gerle (discussed in Chapter 4 above):

Wherefore take a thinne flat ruler of whitish woode, and make it iust as long and straight as from the inward side of the Nut to the inward side of the Bridge, then note that end which you meane to [represent] the Bridge with some small marke, and the other end with the letter *A*, because you may know which belongeth to the one and to the other, then lay the ruler vpon a Table, and take a payre of compasses and seeke out the iust middle of the Ruler . . .[1]

– but with various differences. One of several minor changes is that Dowland's fret positions are marked on the ruler with letters, corresponding to those of French tablature, rather than with numbers (thus fret 1 is B, fret 2 is C, and so on). Frets 8 and 10 are 'one third part from' frets 1 and 3 to the bridge. Fret 9, 'which soundeth *Tonne* cum *diapente*, or an *Hexachordo maior*', was obviously intended to be placed analogously, but a gremlin seems to have put down the letter 'E' instead of 'K' for fret 9, and to have described the position as 'a third part from the Bridge to C' rather than the other way around. The same gremlin evidently substituted 'D' for 'A' in the instructions to put fret 7 at 1/3 of the distance from 12 to the nut, and substituted 'first fret' for 'fifth fret' in the instructions for fret 5.

There is another, more curious error. Fret 3, instead of being placed 5/3 as far from 1 as 1 is from the nut, is placed only half again as far – and this by a remarkably awkward procedure:

diuide the distance from the letter B. to A. in three parts, which being done, measure from the B. vpwards foure times and an halfe, and that wil giue you the third fret, sounding a *Semiditone*: mark that also with a prick, & set thereon the letter D.

The semiditone (minor 3rd) is thus represented by a fret only $15.\overline{15}\%$ (5/33) of the distance from the nut to the bridge, whereas even a pythagorean minor 3rd, the smallest appropriate to any renaissance music, requires theoretically 15.6% (5/32). In equal temperament the distance is some 15.9% $(1 - \sqrt[4]{1/2})$.

1 Dowland 1610: 16; transcribed by David Mitchell in Poulton 1972: 458.

One might doubt whether Dowland saw quite how close to the nut these instructions would put fret 3, since he could have got it there by merely halving the distance to fret 1 and then going down three times that amount from 1 (instead of dividing the distance by 3 and going down ostensibly $4\frac{1}{2}$ times). The $15.\overline{15}\%$ position would serve nicely for a *mi* fret in 1/6-comma meantone temperament (ideally at $15.2\%)^2$ – that is, for G♯ and D♯ on the F and C strings. But most of Dowland's pieces use fret 3 exclusively for *fa* notes, and the minority that use it for *mi* use it for *fa* as well (and usually more prominently, as in Example 17).[3]

Example 17. Dowland, *Semper Dowland, semper dolens* (1974 edition: 42), opening.

Unlike Gerle, Dowland put fret 4 'iust in the middle [between 3 and 5], the which will be a perfect *ditone*'. If fret 3 were really only 5/33 down from the nut, this prescription for fret 4 would indeed give a major 3rd only about one beat per second larger than pure (assuming it to be matched on the open strings and played as a harmonic interval). But here again the method seems too clever: one could get a perfect ditone at fret 4 by merely putting it as 1/5 of the distance from the nut to the bridge, without distorting the position of fret 3.

If the instructions were less problematical we could easily take the term 'perfect ditone' to suggest some form of meantone – but with fret 3 at the wrong enharmonic position for most of Dowland's music! Fret 1 as well

2 Calculated as follows: The *mi* position for fret 3 is a diatonic semitone's worth towards the nut from fret 4. In just intonation this would be $\frac{4}{5} \times \frac{16}{15} = 64/75$ of the distance from the bridge to the nut. In 1/6-comma meantone temperament, the major 3rd is 1/3 comma larger, and the diatonic semitone 1/6 comma smaller (see chapter 4, note 33), so fret 3 is 1/2 comma's worth towards the bridge from its just-intonation position, or $64/75 \div \sqrt{81/80}$ from the bridge to the nut. This is 0.848, or 15.2% of the distance from the nut to the bridge.

3 In the 1974 edition of Dowland's lute music, fret 3 is used for *mi* notes on pp. 1, 2, 4, 9, 11, 14, 51, 53, 64 and 72.

would be poorly placed, as he used it freely for both *mi* and *fa* notes (Example 18). All told, these fretting instructions are so inept that one must doubt whether Dowland ever used them. This doubt is confirmed by the fact that his introductory remarks refer to two ways of placing the frets, by ear and 'by measure', and declare that skilful players used the former:

Now to place these frets aright, whereby wee may make vse of these various sounds by them caused, there is two wayes: the one is the deuine sence of Hearing, which those that be skilfull doe most vse . . . [but] Pithagoras searching after a certaine distance of Interuals, left the iudgement of the Eares, and went on to the rules of Reason: for hee would not giue credit to mans Eares, which are chaunged partly by reason, partly by outward accidents: as for example, let a companie of Lutenists, Violists, &c. which be skilfull; play each after other, and you see euery one as the Instrument cometh to him, Tune according to the iudgement of his own Eare. [Dowland adds that Pythagoras did not have to cope with the vagaries of lute strings; so he discovered the pythagorean ratios.]

Thus the Interuals being found out by waight and number, we will endeauour to set them downe by measure . . .[4]

Example 18. Dowland, *A Fancy* (1974 edition: 24), opening.

4   Dowland 1610: 16.

In Table 1 (p. 8 above), the empty space might have been labelled 'modified meantone' to suggest a combination of uniform semitones and approximately pure major 3rds. If a pure major 3rd is divided into four equal semitones, however, twelve of these semitones will fall about a quarter-tone short of an octave (just as three pure major 3rds do). The discrepancy is called the 'lesser diesis' and amounts to virtually two syntonic commas. According to J. Murray Barbour, the late-renaissance theorist Giovanni Maria Artusi proposed a modified-meantone fretting in which each octave would contain ten uniformly small semitones and two others a comma larger (at frets 4-5 or 11-12).[5] In this system, frets 2, 4, 5, 7, 9, 11 and 12 would be set for a major scale in 1/4-comma meantone temperament, and the open courses tuned accordingly. Frets 1, 3, 6, 8 and 10 would be midway, intervallically, between their alternative enharmonic positions in regular meantone. Within each of the two groups every interval would be the same size as in 1/4-comma meantone; but any interval involving both groups would differ by a comma: octaves, unisons and major 3rds (which are pure in 1/4-comma meantone temperament) would be impure by a comma, while 5ths, 4ths, minor 3rds and major 6ths (all of which are tempered by 1/4 comma in the regular meantone scheme) would be impure by 3/4 or by $1\frac{1}{4}$ comma. An examination of Table 7 will show that among the first five frets, the sour intervals would include the 5ths between frets 3 and 5, and octaves between fret 3 and an open string or fret 5, and most of the 4ths between the middle pair of courses:

Some of these intervals are so routinely encountered (see Example 19, and also the last bars of Examples 3, 13 and 14) that any sensitive player would soon be driven to make corrections, perhaps starting with fret 3.

Artusi did not really advocate this scheme, however. The passage cited by Barbour is about a theory of tempered *vocal* intervals, and Artusi attributed it implicitly to Claudio Monteverdi.

According to the theory, the diminished 4th F♯-B♭ would be made up of two 16:15 semitones (F♯-G and A-B♭) and a minor whole-tone (10:9 for G-A), were not the whole-tone rendered pythagorean

16:15 less   9:8   16:15 less
½ comma   (10:9 × 81:80)   ½ comma

5   Barbour 1951: 146-48.

by taking half a comma from each of the semitones. This would involve dividing the comma according to 'the doctrine of Ludovico Fogliani' (see Figure 7 on p. 27 above). Meanwhile the semitones, in giving away a half-comma each, would become exactly half the size of the 9:8 whole-tone.

Table 7. Note names at the various fingering positions (if the outer courses are named G) in the 'modified meantone' scheme attributed by Barbour to Artusi.

nut	fret 1	2	3	4	5	6	7	
G	G♯/A♭	A	A♯/B♭	B	C	C♯/D♭	D	
D	D♯/E♭	E	E♯/F♭	F♯♯	G	G♯/A♭	A	
A	A♯/B♭	B	B♯/C♭	C♯♯	D	D♯/E♭	E	etc.
F	F♯/G♭	G	G♯/A♭	A	B♭	B♯/C♭	C	
C	C♯/D♭	D	D♯/E♭	E	F	F♯/G♭	G	
G	G♯/A♭	A	A♯/B♭	B	C	C♯/D♭	D	

Example 19. Anonymous, *Calleno custure me* from William Ballet's lute book (transcribed as the first piece in Harwood 1962), conclusion.

In describing and criticizing this theory Artusi used a number of phrases and statements – 'Ludovico Fogliani's doctrine'; 'one must ascertain half of the 81:80 comma, because by such a quantity the 10:9 is smaller than the 9:8'; 'divide the whole-tone into two equal parts'; etc. – which together may have given Barbour the mistaken impression that he was proposing to divide Fogliani's mean tone (a half-comma larger than 10:9 and smaller than 9:8) into two equal semitones. But actually Artusi favoured equal temperament, 'according to the view of Aristoxenus', on the lute and chitarrone; and the semitones of the theory itself also approximate to equal temperament. Artusi's criticism amounts to hardly more than metaphysical quibbling, and the real significance of the passage is that Monteverdi appears to have countenanced the singing of his madrigals in a kind of intonation indistinguishable, for all practical purposes, from equal temperament.

The passage in question is the ninth *consideratione* in Artusi's *Considerationi musicali* (1603).[6]

At the outset Artusi says that in his previous criticism (1600) of 'certain modern composers' he had not named anyone, hoping that this tact would induce them to admit their errors rationally. The examples of music cited by Artusi in 1600 have been identified and suggest that all these composers were really one and the same person, Claudio Monteverdi;[7] nevertheless Artusi says now that 'some' of them, guided by capricious humours, not only failed to change their views, but went from bad to worse. (In fact Artusi had been sending letters, 'full of benevolence and civility', to Monteverdi, who 'instead of answering in the same manner, made reply through a third person, and [in] letters without his own name'.[8] The letters were signed 'l'Ottuso Accademico' – a wicked use of assonance and mock self-deprecation to stigmatize poor Artusi himself.)

Presently Artusi's syntax breaks down in the course of an elaborate simile about an artist who thinks he is depicting 'a well-made figure, . . . proportioned in its parts', but is really representing a monster such as is described in book V [sic] of the *Aeneid*.[9] (The rhetorical effect would be more impressive if Artusi's own sentence were coherent.) On his way out of the simile Artusi gives us a concise summary of the musical monstrosities to be discovered in the work of these wretched composers:

Il che imitano benissimo questi tali   Which [monster] they imitate very well,
quando nel mezo delle loro cantilene,   when in the middle of their songs,

---

6   Artusi 1603: 29-33.   7   Palisca 1968: 134-35.
8   Artusi 1608: 6. 'Sig. Claudio hebbe all'hora il torto lui; perche quando l'Artusi gli scrisse quelle lettere, gli le scrisse piene d'amoreuolezza e ciuiltà; & egli in vece di rispondergli nella istessa maniera, gli fece rispondere per vna terza persona, & lettere senza nome proprio.' On the same page Artusi's fictitious spokesman 'Braccino' threatens 'on a better occasion' to publish 'le lettere, le copie di cui sono nelle mani mie, & debbono ancora essere nelle mani del Sig. Monteverde'. However the letters to 'Ottuso' were actually drafted, there is no evidence that the views they expressed were distinct from those of the composer they defended.
9   Artusi says 'quinto', but the lines cited are from book III (216-18).

nel principio, & nel fine ci rapportano	at the beginning, and at the end they set out
interualli sgarbatissimi da modulare;	very ungraceful intervals to perform;
nella pouertà dell'Harmonia;	in the poverty of the harmony;
nella lontananza tal uolta delle parti,	in having the voices sometimes too far apart
gl'estremi di cui se ne giungono	(their extremes reach
fino alle 23. Voci;	as far as twenty-three diatonic steps);
nella poca osseruanza de modi;	in their slight regard for the modes;
nella positione, & ordine delle	in placing and ordering the
consonantie, lontana dalle buone Regole;	consonances [in a manner] alien to good rules;
nella mala imitatione delle parole,	[and] in the poor imitation of the words,
come si può uedere nel principio	as one can see at the beginning
della Cantilena di sopra posta,	of the song given above,
che dice, Ma se con la pietà.	which says 'Ma se con la pietà',
L'Harmonia di cui più tosto moue	the harmony of which would move [one] sooner
à risa, che à pietà . . .	to laughter than to pity.

'Poor imitation of the words' – can *this* be Monteverdi? Indeed; the example cited is from the second part of *Ecco Silvio*, later published in his fifth book (1605) of madrigals (see Example 20).[10] Now we reach the heart of the matter: the real cause of all these bad composers' faults is their reliance upon intuition rather than science (so venerable was Boethius' precept that the true musician, 'weighing reason, claims the science of song not by the servitude of work but by the authority of speculation').[11] And the proof? – their absurd theory of certain chromatic intervals.

Example 20. Monteverdi, *Ma se con la pietà* (1605), opening.

10   In addition to the apparently balletto-like rhythm, I suppose Artusi disapproved of placing the weak syllables 'la' and '-za' on strong beats. For a modern discussion see Razzi 1980: 306-09.
11   Boethius, *De institutione musica*: book I, ch. 34 ('ratione perpensa canendi scientiam non servitio operis sed imperio speculationis adsumpsit').

In modern terms, the theory's diminished 4th, with the ratio $512{:}405$ ($=\frac{16}{15}\cdot\frac{16}{15_3}\cdot\frac{16}{9}^2$), would amount to 406 cents ($\log\frac{512}{405}\div\frac{\log 2}{1200}$). This is slightly less than the pythagorean major 3rd or 'ditone'($\frac{9}{8}\cdot\frac{9}{8}=\frac{81}{64}$), which amounts to 408 cents ($\log\frac{81}{64}\div\frac{\log 2}{1200}$). The discrepancy is in the direction of the 400-cent major 3rd of equal temperament (which is also of course a diminished 4th).

The quantitative assertion to which Artusi takes particular exception is that if the 16:15 diatonic semitone (nearly 112 cents) were to give up half a comma (half of some 22 cents), the resulting 101-cent semitone would amount to half of the 9:8 whole-tone (that is, half of 204 cents), which in fact it misses by only one cent, and again in the direction of the equal-temperament equivalent.[12]

Of course diminished 4ths were stock in trade for Monteverdi in his chromatic moments. One need only think of the concluding section ('Per far che moia...') of *Ah dolente partita*, the first madrigal in his *Quarto libro* (1603). Example 21 shows a diminished 4th in the peroration to that chromatic *tour de force* at the end of the fourth book, *Piagne e sospira*.

The theory (as reported by Artusi) also gave a special status to C♯-B♭: not really a 7th, nor a 6th, but nonetheless a good sound. Prominent diminished 7ths are rare in Monteverdi's music, but the few I have noticed are between C♯ and B♭. Examples 22*a* and *b* are from *Orfeo* and *Arianna.*

For his part Artusi approved of equal temperament on the lute and chitarrone, but 'according to the view of Aristoxenus' – that is, without numbers. Elsewhere he had expressed the hope that theorists might find a satisfactory formulation of equal temperament ('proportioni tali, che fra di loro siano eguali'),[13] but his attack on what appears to have been Monteverdi's theory

Example 21. Monteverdi, *Piagne e sospira* (1603), first appearance of the concluding verse.

---

12   More exactly: $\log\frac{16}{15}\div\frac{\log 2}{1200}=111.73$; half of ($\log\frac{81}{80}\div\frac{\log 2}{1200}$) is 10.75; and the difference between these is 100.98; whereas half of ($\log\frac{9}{8}\div\frac{\log 2}{1200}$) is 101.96.

13   Artusi 1600: 31[r.]

Example 22. Diminished 7ths in Monteverdi's *Orfeo* (1609: act 2 scene 1) and the *Lamento d'Arianna* (1614). Other extant versions of the lament (first performed monodically, in 1608) show the same use of C♯-B♭ (1961 edition: 21 and 40).

shows that he felt they mustn't do it with irrational numbers.[14] Although Artusi could give no formula for equal temperament, he said that the intervals had a 'pre-fixed terminus' on 'the artificially made instrument'. He did not actually say whether they could be tuned by ear (as Dowland tuned them) or must be set out by geometry, as his own teacher Zarlino had shown how to do (see Figure 6 on p. 26 above). But Artuis did say that the voice could not justly divide the whole-tone into two equal parts; he described the diminished 7th and diminished 4th as 'false for singing' (though he approved implicitly of Marenzio's use of a diminished 7th in his madrigal *Falsa credenza*, as shown in Example 23); and he declared that the natural voice could not negotiate so unnatural an interval as the diminished 4th by means of a natural 3rd. Of course 'natural' is always a slippery word and often a source of obfuscation; but clearly Artusi felt that singers could never gauge an interval by sheer magnitude,[15] and he implied that the irrational numbers

14   Of course that is the kind one needs, in this case $\sqrt[12]{2}$. Here again Artusi was indebted to Boethius, who had (as we have seen: cf. p. 20 above) assigned 'magnitudes' to geometry and astronomy and thereby excluded them from the science of music, which he said dealt with relations between 'multitudes'. (On irrational numbers, see p. 31 above, note 36.)

15   In this respect he was no Aristoxenian: see p. 30 above.

Example 23. Marenzio, *Falsa credenza havete donna* (1586), beginning.

latent in the theory under attack – the square roots of 81/80 and of 9/8 – prove that Monteverdi had no 'rational' understanding of music. Here is an abbreviated version of the passage, starting after the list of monstrosities translated above:

Tutto questo disordine
da altro non nasce, se non che
non intendono altro
che quello che gli capricij loro
le dicono, che stij bene; però
ci rapportano interualli tall'hora,
che loro stessi non li conoscono,
dicono però che sono cose noue,
se ben sono più uecchie, che
il Cucco; come li seguenti,
il primo de quali dicono, che non è ne
sesta, ne settima, ma che consona
benissimo alle sue orecchie,
che sono purgate.

All this disorder
stems from nothing other than that
they understand nothing other
than that which their caprices
tell them will be all right. For
they sometimes set us out intervals
which they themselves do not know,
and say that they are something new
even though they are older than
the cuckoo-bird: like the following,
the first of which, they say, is neither
a 6th nor a 7th, but resounds
very well to their ears,
which are purged.

Interualli
per cantare falsi,
ma per sonare
ne lauti buoni.

Intervals
false for singing,
but good for
playing on lutes.

Il secondo uogliono, che
sia una terza, ouero Decima . . .
contenuta da due semituoni . . .
di proportione sesquiquindecima,
e 'l tuono
che nel mezo uiene ad esserui posto,
sia di proportione sesquinona,
ma che però col mezo, & ordine
della Dottrina di Ludouico Fogliani,
uogliono leuare dall'uno e l'altro
semituono tanta quantità, che
il tuono per tale accrescimento

They hold that the second [interval]
is a 3rd, or rather 10th,
containing two semitones
in the proportion 16:15,
and that the whole-tone
located in the middle
is in the proportion 10:9
– except that by the method and system
of Ludovico Fogliani's doctrine
they would remove from each of the two
semitones a certain quantity so that
the whole-tone by this increase

diuenghi sesquiottauo,	would become 9:8,
& gli semituoni restino	and the semitones remain
fra di loro eguali,	equal to each other,
e per la metà del tuono.	and to half of the whole-tone.
Quanto al primo interuallo, dico,	As for the first interval, I say
non è cosa noua, perche fu usato	it is not a new thing since it was used
da Luca Marenzio nel principio d'un	by Luca Marenzio at the beginning of a
suo madrigale, le parole di cui	madrigal of his, the words of which
dicono: falsa credenza, per dimonstrar	are 'False belief', to demonstrate
apunto un'interuallo falso nelle voci,	indeed an interval false for voices
& nella modulatione, ma non è falso	and in harmony, but not false
nel lauto, & nel chitarone . . . perche	on the lute or chitarrone – because
nel luogo istesso, che il Sonatore	in the same place that the player
pone le dita per farci sentire	puts his fingers to make us hear
una sesta, le pone ancora à farci	a 6th, he puts them again to make us
intendere questo interuallo . . .	perceive this interval . . .
diuidendo il tuono in due	dividing the whole-tone into two
semituoni eguali . . .	equal semitones . . .
Quanto alla Consideratione di questo	As for the
secondo interuallo, . . . il Sonatore	second interval, . . . the player
porrà nello' istesso luogo le dita	will put his fingers in the same place
per farci sentire la terza naturale	to make us hear a natural 3rd . . . .
. . . Ma la uoce naturale non auezza	But the natural voice is not suited
à modulare	to negotiate
simili interualli, non naturali,	such unnatural intervals
per interualli naturali, . . .	by means of natural ones, . . .
non hauendo prefisso termine	not having a preset stopping place
come l'instromento fatto dall'Arte	like an artificial instrument.
. . . non può giustamente diuidire	. . . It cannot justly divide
il tuono in due parte eguali . . .	the whole-tone into two equal parts . . .
Ma intorno à quello che dicono di	And as for what they say about
leuare tanto all'uno de semituoni,	subtracting as much from one semitone,
quanto all'altro per accomodare	as from the other, to accommodate
il tuono sesquinono,	the 10:9 whole-tone
acciò diuenti sesquiottauo,	(thereby rendered 9:8)
con certi, & determinati	with known and specified
numeri rationali, bisognerà prima	rational numbers, one must first
ritrouare la metà del	ascertain half of the
Comma sesquiottantessimo, perche	81:80 comma, because
di tanta quantità il	by such a quantity the
sesquinono è minore del sesquiottauo.	10:9 is smaller than the 9:8;
la qual metà conosciuta potrassi	when that half is known you can
poi leuare dall'uno, e l'altro de	then subtract [it] from each of the
semituoni, è aggiungerla al tuono,	semitones and add it to the whole-tone,
che all'hora farà il tuono sesquinono	which will then convert the 10:9 whole-tone
diuentato sesquiottauo . . .	into 9:8 . . . [But]
Due cosi quiui ci sono da considerare	two things should be considered here:
. . . La prima, che gl'inuentori di	. . . first, that the inventors of
cosi fatte spropositate	such ill-conceived proposals . . .
. . . non potranno mai diuidere la	will never be able to divide the
proportio sesquiottantessima . . .	81:80 proportion

in due parte eguali, con certi, & determinati numeri rationali. La seconda è, che . . . impossibile è, che quel residuo delli due semituoni restino per la metà del tuono sesquiottauo; Essendo conclusione firmissima nelle Mathematiche, che nissuna proportione superparticolare possi essere diuisa in due parte eguali con certi & determinati numeri rationali . . . Et perche io ho promesso di dimonstrare vna sfilzata d'interualli forastieri, non conosciuti da quelli che essercitano questa moderna confusione, interualli inutili da cantare, con le voci nelle cantilene ordinarie, se bene sono è saranno conosciuti da quelli che suonano il Lauto, Chitarone, & altri cosi fatti instromenti; gli ponerò qua di sotto ordinatamente . . . considerando il tuono diuiso in due semituoni eguali . . . come si vede nel Lauto . . . & è secondo la mente di Aristosseno appunto. Adunque la seconda minore, è lo istesso semituono. La seconda maggiore, è . . . di due semituoni composto. La terza minore . . . di tre . . .	into two equal parts with known and specified rational numbers, [and] secondly, that it is impossible that the residuum of [each of] the two semitones would amount to half of the 9:8 whole-tone. For it is a very firm conclusion in mathematics that no superparticular proportion can be divided into two equal parts with known and specified rational numbers.[16] . . . But since I have promised to demonstrate a series of surd intervals unknown to those who exercise this modern confusion – intervals useless for vocal performance in songs of a normal kind, even though they are and will remain known to those who play the lute, chitarrone, and other instruments made in that way – I put them in order here below . . . regarding the whole-tone [as being] divided into two equal semitones . . . as one sees on the lute . . . and this follows the view, indeed, of Aristoxenus. Now then, the minor 2nd is the semitone itself; the major 2nd is . . . composed of two semitones; the minor 3rd . . . of three [etc.].

16   A 'superparticular proportion' is a proportion between two integers one of which equals the other plus 1. Artusi's point is rather weak, as the theory does not imply that any rational numbers *should* be associated with a half-comma or with the semitones in question.

7 Conclusions

The history which we have surveyed illustrates very well that music theory embraces a wealth of metaphysical absurdities (Bartolus), garbled plagiarisms (Dowland), eccentric proposals (Salmon) and the like. No less remarkable, however, is the information of practical value which may be extracted from the evidence surveyed in this book. Here is a brief summary.

As far as music specifically for lute or viol is concerned, the use of an instrument fretted for equal temperament is never historically 'wrong'. Remarks by Spataro, Agricola, Cardano and Vicentino show that some players used equal semitones even before 1550. After that date equal temperament became, in most theorists' opinion, normal for fretted instruments (though only later for keyboard instruments).

For all practical purposes the best and historically the most likely rule for an equal-temperament fretting is simply to shorten the distance to the bridge by 1/18 for each successive fret.

Precisely how a good player may shade the tuning of such an instrument, however, is quite another matter. Aron, Praetorius and an 'impostor' friend of Doni are among those who remarked upon the fretted instruments' flexibility of intonation. In a viol consort it is perfectly legitimate – indeed delightful – to cultivate justly intoned chords. (Every first-rate group which I have heard does so.) In a renaissance or early-baroque ensemble with harpsichord or organ, it would be better for the fretted instruments to follow the proper meantone tuning of the keyboard instruments than for the latter to be tuned in equal temperament: if music of that period does require equal temperament, it was almost certainly not intended for keyboard instruments.[1]

On the *basse de viole* accompanied by the harpsichord in a high-baroque *tempérament ordinaire*, particular care should be taken to match the harpsi-

1 John Bull's famous 'Ut-Re-Mi-Fa-Sol-La' (no. 51 in the Fitzwilliam Virginal Book) was originally not for equal temperament but for a keyboard instrument with the strings or pipes disposed to provide enharmonic alternatives (as indicated by the fact that those sections which use flats are devoid of sharps, and vice versa).

chord's intonation at least insofar as good ensemble requires: Marais, for instance, appears to have done so. To this end if it helps to shift fret 4 slightly towards the nut, contemporary French fretting instructions (Danoville, Jean Rousseau) are quite vague enough to allow this licence.

Remarks by Bermudo, Ganassi, Dowland and Jean Rousseau suggest that many good players adjusted the frets by ear (as they often do today) rather than conform to an exactly regular spacing. Such *ad hoc* irregularities might be used to facilitate some style of intonation with 3rds less heavily tempered than in equal temperament (that is, with fret 4 slightly closer to the nut), but they must not go beyond one's capacity to produce a pure unison or octave wherever the music requires. Historically inclined players should bear in mind, in this connection, that the irregular schemes which have been attributed to Ganassi and Artusi are chimeras of mistaken scholarship. Ganassi's 'geometry' was intended merely to prescribe where the frets should be tied before being adjusted to their true positions by informal rules of thumb and by ear. Artusi was describing a purely abstract scheme by which his enemy, Monteverdi, appears to have sanctioned the singing of his madrigals in equal temperament (which in fact was the only system Artusi himself approved of for lutes and viols).

Just-intonation fretting schemes (with a distinction for two sizes of wholetone) remained always a matter of theory and experiment, never of common practice.

Pythagorean frettings (based exclusively on 3:2, 4:3 and 9:8) may have been used in high-gothic and early-renaissance times, but we have no repertory specifically for lute or viol from which to prove this. The Attaingnant preludes of 1529, which I examined on account of Fine's contemporary pythagorean fretting scheme, are not well served by pythagorean intonation.

Finally, an instrument fretted for some form of meantone temperament may be the most appropriate, historically as well as aesthetically, for some music from the first half of the sixteenth century. This seems particularly promising for the music of Arnolt Schlick and Luis Milán.

APPENDIX 1

Tablature notation

Some renaissance viol music and nearly all music written for the lute is written in a kind of notation that does not tell the player the names of the notes but instead indicates which string is to be played at which fret (if any). For instance, Example 24 shows Ganassi's tuning checks, from which Example 1 (p. 7, above) is taken. The 'C' at the beginning of each *Essempio* is a

Example 24. Ganassi's tuning checks for the viol (1543: ch. 6).

Eſſempio

Eſſempio.

conventional sign for the metrical framework of the rhythm; in modern terms it means 'common time', with four beats to the bar. The ubiquitous (J and ʔ signs are fermatas, equivalent to the modern ◡ and ⌒. (It exemplifies Ganassi's liking for incoherent redundancy that he should indicate 'common time' when in fact all the notes are indefinitely long!) The other signs are numbers, namely:

 and

Each horizontal line represents one of the instrument's six strings, and each number tells which fret to use. A zero means to play the open string. Hence in the first *Essempio* the second note is five semitones – that is, a perfect 4th – higher than the first note. We know this without knowing the pitch of either note: as far as the tablature tells us, the music may be played indifferently well on a bass or treble viol, and the pitch level of a given instrument may be adjusted at will (within feasible limits) to draw a certain quality of sound from the instrument, or to accommodate a singer or match some other instrument lacking in such flexibility.

For all the examples of tablature in this book (except the cittern chords in Example 16) the intervals among the open strings are the same:

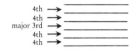

Ganassi's tablature shows the influence of the lute in that the top line represents the string that is lowest in pitch, the bottom line represents the string highest in pitch, and the others are arranged accordingly in between. (On a lute the courses are arranged this way physically, the string highest in pitch being the one closest to the player's lap.) In Ganassi's first *Essempio*

the 0 on the second line ⸗ makes a unison with the 5 on the first line ⸗

the 0 on the third line ⸗ makes a unison with the 5 on the second line ⸗

the 7 on the second line ⸗ makes an octave with the 0 on the first line ⸗

and so on.

To transcribe from tablature to staff notation, one must choose, arbitrarily or conventionally, a set of hypothetical letter-names for the open strings. It is only when the outer courses are named G, D or A, however, that all six lines of the tablature will represent 'naturals'.

	C	G	D	A	E
4th	F	C	G	D	A
4th	B♭	F	C	G	D
major 3rd	D	A	E	B	F♯
4th	G	D	A	E	B
4th	C	G	D	A	E

Scholars often refer to these as the G, D and A 'tunings', but it would be more precise to regard them as mere differences of nomenclature. Since

French music for the baroque *basse de viole* was written in staff notation implying the D nomenclature (see Examples 6 and 7), this seems the most convenient choice for Ganassi's tablature. Thus his tuning checks may be transcribed as in Example 25.

Example 25. Ganassi's tuning checks for the viol.

Lute music is usually transcribed according to the G or A nomenclature.

In Luis Milán's *El maestro* every piece is labelled as being in a particular *tono* or mode, and the labels always imply the A nomenclature. The top line of Milán's tablature represents the string that is highest in pitch:

In France and England, stylized letters were used instead of numbers:

open string	fret 1	fret 2	fret 3	fret 4	fret 5 etc.
a	b	c	q	e	f

and we find the letters written directly above the line rather than being intersected by it. As in Milán's tablature, the lines correspond to the relative pitch of the strings rather than to their physical position on the instrument.

In sixteenth-century German tablature there are no horizontal lines, and different signs are used for the same positions on different strings. Figure 21 shows the signs used in Arnolt Schlick's music (see Example 15).

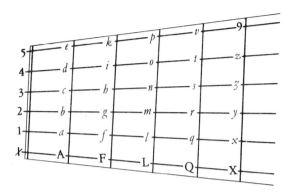

Figure 21

Obviously the arrangement of the numbers and small letters dates back to a time when the instrument had only five courses. All the sources that use this system share these older signs, but there is considerable variation in the signs employed for the added bass course.

Finally, in all these systems of tablature the rhythmic signs are written above the signs for pitch, and they never indicate how long the sound of a note is to last (in reality the sound will fade rather quickly on the lute in any case) but merely how soon one should play the next note of the composition. If a note or chord has no rhythmic sign over it, the duration (in this sense of the term) is the same as for the previous note or chord.

1   See Apel 1942: 54-81.

APPENDIX 2

Some pertinent music not for fretted instruments

Willaert's *Quidnam ebrietas*

Artusi is our main source for Willaert's 'cantilena a due voci' which he said
was entitled *Quidnam ebrietas*. In Example 26, words have been applied
from a passage in Horace's Epistle 5 (book I) which appears to be the text
Willaert had in mind:

Quid non ebrietas dissignat?	What does drunkenness not achieve?
Operta recludit,	It discloses secrets,
Spes iubet esse ratas,	orders hopes to be fulfilled,
ad proela trudit inertem,	drives the timid into battle,
Sollicitis animis onus eximit,	removes the burden from anxious minds,
addocet artes.	and teaches the arts.
Fecundi calices quem non fecere disertum?	Full cups – whom have they not made eloquent?

I have placed in round brackets a number of accidentals not in the original,
assuming that in the first half of the piece each new flat becomes part of
the signature, as it were, and that G♭ wants C♭ for its *fa* in bar 20. Then in
the second half, as if to confirm that drunkennness 'removes the burden
from anxious minds', all the tenor's notes are lowered one degree
diatonically.[1] Apart from all this, an F and three C's are sharped at
cadences in keeping with normal performing practice at the time.

Willaert appears to have composed a four-part version of this piece, and
although the bass has been lost, Edward Lowinsky has used the surviving
alto part to devise a reconstruction (see Example 27).

Louis Couperin's F♯ minor Pavane

In the first section of Louis Couperin's F♯ minor Pavane for harpsichord
(Example 28), nearly every point at which the composer has either used or
evaded a D♯, A♯, E♯ or B♯ will betray, in performance, a precise sense of
how these notes are inflected in the kind of irregular tuning which soon
became normal on the *clavecin*: gradually our capacity is built up to

---

1 Levitan 1936-8 discusses alternative possibilities.

Example 26. Willaert, *Quid non ebrietas* (1519), cantus and tenor (Artusi 1600: 21; text underlay after Lowinsky 1956-8).

Example 27. Willaert, *Quid non ebrietas* (1519), opening of the four-part version (with the bass reconstructed by Lowinsky (1956-8)).

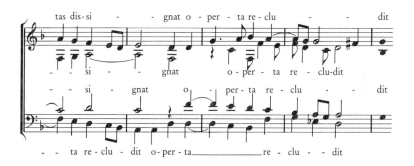

endure their rapid beating and melodic weirdness until at the double-bar we can just tolerate the unmitigated E♯. Attentive performers will notice the evasions of E♯ in bar 2 and B♯ in bar 5; the sly introduction, at bar 8, of A♯ in the bass (where its melodic quality as a leading-note will be evident, but where at the same time its overtones have precious little opportunity to beat with those of the other notes in the chord); the 'covering' of E♯ by the A's in bars 10, 11 and 16, and of A♯ by D in bar 12; the use of low B at the end of bar 13 where its effect is to halve the rate of beating

Example 28. Louis Couperin, F♯ minor Pavane (1936 edition: 121-22).

which otherwise would be exposed in the major 10th B-D♯; the remarkable way in which the beating of the G♯'s in bars 6 and 13-14 enriches the sonority; and other such effects. The chromaticism of this composition is governed throughout by a fine regard for the nuances of the tuning, and this may well have been one aspect of those 'learned researches' which Jean Le Gallois in 1680 attributed to Louis Couperin in his work as a composer.[2]

2   See Fuller 1976: 25.

Some geometrical devices

A

The mesolabe. Having described this device in 1558, Zarlino explained in 1571 how it could be used specifically to find two geometrical means between a pair of given string lengths. Figure 22 is from the later account. The rectangles *defg*, *hikl* and *mnop* represent the three sliding frames; *ab* and *cb* represent the given lengths (notice that in this case the mesolabe has been constructed to be as high as the monochord string *ab* is long); and *dt* represents, in effect, an elastic straight-edge whose angle can be varied by sliding *t* along the base. According to Zarlino's explanation, one begins by 'placing the three parallelograms *defg*, *hikl* and *mnop* one under the other, as you see; . . . then make the third parallelogram's side *po* . . . equal to the string [segment] *cb* at point *s*, and arrange the others [*hikl*,

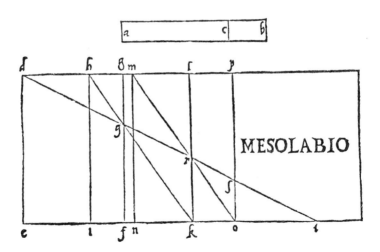

Figure 22. Zarlino's diagram of a mesolabe whose height is equal to a given string length (1571: 163). (The letter *q*, between *d* and *r* on the diagonal *dt*, looks very like a *g* in the original.)

mnop and *dt*] in such a way that [while *dt* passes through *s*] the diagonals *kh* and *mo* meet the sides *gf* and *lk* at points *q* and *r* [i.e. intersecting *dt*]. From which the two mean lengths *qf* and *rk* are born.'

B

An anonymous Hellenic method, described by Athanasius Kircher in 1650, for finding two geometric means with a pair of nested L-squares (Figure 23). Mark off the given lengths AB and AC along two perpendicular lines, and then place the L-squares as shown, so that while one touches B and the other C, the extended lines cut through the right angles which the L-squares make at D and E. The logical proof for this method is very simple: BD and CE are parallel, so the triangles which they form with A have the same three angles and are therefore similar. The remaining triangle is also similar, because each of its acute angles complements one of the acute angles of the other triangles. Hence the ratios AC:AE:AD:AB are all equal.

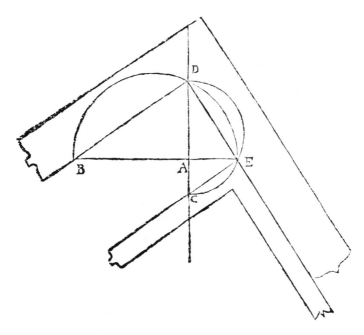

Figure 23. Kircher's illustration of a method for finding two geometric means with a pair of L-squares 1650: I, 205).

C

A method with straight-edge and compass, which I have simplified from a construction attributed to Nicomedes by Lemme Rossi in 1666.[1]

1. Draw a line about half again as long as the sounding string, mark off the string length, and find its midpoint (B). Set the compass at that length (AB):

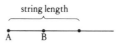

2. Find point C equidistant from A and B; draw a line from C through B; and draw its perpendicular from B as shown:

3. 'Hinge' a straight-edge at C and swing it until DE (as shown) is equal to the compass span (AB); mark points D and E:

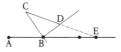

Now BE is the length from fret 4 to the bridge (and CD the length from fret 8).

D

A simple method for 18:17 semitones, derived from Zarlino's *Sopplimenti musicali* (see Figure 24). This is so compact it can be drawn on the fingerboard.

1. Not very far from one edge of the fingerboard draw a perpendicular from the nut towards the bridge; mark off a point 18 inches from the bridge; and draw a perpendicular across the fingerboard at that point:

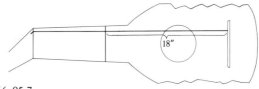

1   Rossi 1666: 95-7.

2. Mark off 1 inch on this new line and draw a diagonal through this point to the nut as shown:

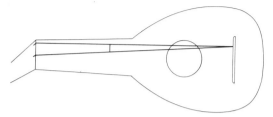

3. The segment you have marked off along the nut equals the distance to fret 1. Transfer it to your original line by turning a compass through some 90°, and then draw the perpendicular at that point:

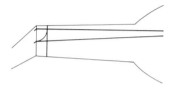

4. Follow suit for each successive fret:

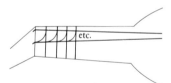

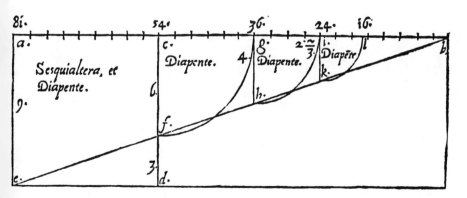

Figure 24. A method published by Zarlino for generating a geometric series of lengths from a given pair of lengths (1588: 183).

Appendix 3

This procedure can be 'adapted' to the $\sqrt[12]{2}$ rule as follows:

1. Draw your straight line from the nut towards the bridge; measure off *along the nut* the distance for fret 1; and draw the diagonal as shown:

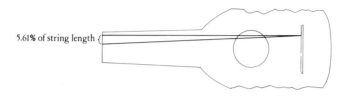

5.61% of string length {

2. Place the frets as shown in step 4 above.

Lute design and the art of proportion

BY GERHARD C. SÖHNE

Surviving works of art show that the classic form of in the European lute was developed during the decades around 1500. It is no coincidence that music theorists first addressed the problems of temperament at the same time, as both innovations served to adapt the instrument to solo polyphony. The number of strings was increased to provide six courses instead of five, and these were now plucked directly by the fingers because the plectrum was too rudimentary for a polyphonic texture. For this new, more ambitious and sophisticated musical use the instrument wanted a new, altogether lighter structure.

No doubt the problems of structural and acoustical refinement which had to be met during this development were solved by trial and error. Then as now, however, such experimentation is likely to involve certain underlying assumptions. We might expect to find the design and acoustical conception of the renaissance lute governed by the same pythagorean mentality which permeated contemporary theories of music, art and architecture alike. (Here I use the term 'pythagorean' in a broader sense than Mark Lindley has done in Chapter 2 above, to refer to the tradition of considering numerical relationships to be the essence of reality.[1]) That is exactly what we do find in the one renaissance text on instruments which shows us a craftsman's way of thinking: the manuscript treatise of Henri Arnaut (c1440).[2]

Arnaut's lute design (see Figure 25) is based upon a circle of which the diameter forms the width of the body. The upper part of the outline is derived from segments of three additional circles which have their centre points at the sides and top of the original circle. The four circles glide into each other.

To place the supporting ribs on the inside of the face, Arnaut divided into eight parts the distance from the centre of the original circle to the upper edge of the outline. Both in the drawing and in his accompanying text, he

---

1 Münxelhaus 1976 surveys medieval pythagoreanism.
2 See Harwood 1960.

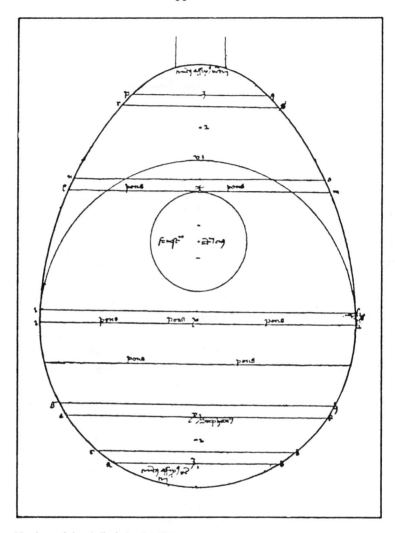

Figure 25. Arnaut's lute belly design (*c*1440).

equated five of these parts to the radius of the circle. This is mathematically inexact. In his geometrical construction the distance from the centre of the original circle to the top of the outline is bound to be numerically incommensurate with the radius of the circle. (If one of the lengths is stated as a rational number, the other requires an irrational number.[3]) Specifically, it can be calculated that Arnaut's geometrical construction should yield a dis-

---

3   See note 36 on p. 31 above for an explanation of one class of irrational numbers.

tance, from the level of maximum width to the top, of $3 - \sqrt{2}$, or some 1.586, times the radius; whereas the 8:5 ratio would make it 1.6 times.

Furthermore, Arnaut said the bridge was to be placed at 1/6 of the height of the face, and the rose midway between the bridge and the top (which would centre it at 7/12 of the height); yet in the drawing the centre of the rose is midway between the second and third of his eight parts (which is slightly less than 7/12 of the height). And again: he said the diameter of the rose was to be 1/3 of the width of the face (at that level), yet in the drawing he used the eightfold division instead, with the rose touching the first and fourth division points.

Three times, therefore, Arnaut indulged in a mathematical inexactitude by implicitly equating three elements of his geometrically constructed outline – its length, its maximum width, and its width at the level of the rose – to some exact multiple of a module (in this case a fraction of the distance from the widest level to the top). By taking these liberties he made his geometrical design answer to the pythagorean concept of numerical proportion. Vitruvius, the ancient Roman authority on architecture, had dwelt upon this concept and said that proportion meant nothing other than the conformity of all the separate parts of the building with one basic module.[4] Much of his *De architectura* was unknown during the middle ages, but it was revived in the fifteenth century and had a great influence upon contemporary architects and architectural theorists. Leon Battista Alberti, 'the Florentine Vitruvius',[5] may exemplify this trend to govern the construction by a scheme of numerical proportions. He wrote:

Finitio quidem apud nos est	Indeed, for us *finitio* is
correspondentia quaedam	a certain correspondence,
linearum inter se / quibus	among themselves, of the lines by which
quantitates dimetiantur.	the quantities are measured.
Earum una est longitudinis: altera	One of these is for the length; another
latitudinis: tertia altitudinis.	for the width; a third for the height.
. . . affirmo illud Pytagorae.	. . . I affirm the [opinion] of Pythagoras:
Certissimum est naturam	it is most certain [that] nature
in omnibus sui esse persimilem.	is consistent in all her [manifestations].
. . . Hi quidem numeri per quos	. . . Indeed, those numbers through which
fiat ut vocum illa concinnitas	it happens that the harmony of voices
auribus gratissima reddatur/	is rendered most pleasing to the ears –
iidem ipsi numeri perficiunt/	those same numbers bring it about
ut oculi animusque	that the eyes and the soul
uoluptate mirifica compleantur.	are filled with a marvellous pleasure.
Ex musicis igitur quibus	Therefore from musicians, by whom
ii talis numeris exploratissimi sunt	such numbers have been much explored,

4   Vitruvius *c* 1486 edition: book III, ch. 1, 1.   5   Grayson 1960: 706.

... tota finitionis ratio	... the entire law of *finitio*
producetur.	is deduced.[6]

Nearly three centuries later Ernst Gottlieb Baron described lute-making in rather similar terms:

... dieweil das gantze Haupt-Wesen	... for the whole essence
wohl auf einem Meister ankommet, der	really stems from a master who
die mathematischen Proportionen,	has taken to heart
welche darzu gehörig,	the mathematical proportions
wohl innen habe,	which pertain thereto,
damit sich die Cavitäten, Höhe,	whereby the spaces, height,
Tieffe, Länge und Breite	depth, length and breadth
recht egal gegen einander verhalten,	interact with each other in equal measure.
welche Egalité denn Ursache ist,	For this 'equalness' is the reason
dass ein Instrument, es mag von	that an instrument, whether it be of
Italiänischen, Teutschen oder	Italian, German or
Französischen &c. Holtze seyn,	French wood,
wohl klinge.	[will] sound well.[7]

More important from a practical point of view than the mystical character of this pythagorean doctrine is the fact that the modular system makes it easy to communicate structural and acoustical data, and thus to create or sustain a tradition. Arnaut's prescription that the bridge of a lute should be placed at 1/6 of the length of the face crops up nearly two hundred years later in Mersenne's *Harmonie universelle*.[8] His rule that the diameter of the rose should be 1/3 of the breadth of the face can be observed in many extant renaissance lutes. As for the little discrepancies between Arnaut's scheme of proportions and his geometry, perhaps he might have said, if someone had called them to his attention, that an expert maker could modify something by 'a small and hidden amount', or that 'with his discretion and diligence he should seek to obviate the slight discrepancy' (see above, pp. 27 and 21).

No lutes from Arnaut's day are preserved, but thanks to the realism of certain artists – painters, South German sculptors, Italian artists in intarsia – we can complement Arnaut's information with other evidence. Figure 26 shows a wooden sculpture of Pythagoras, from a choir stall in Ulm Cathedral, by Jörg Syrlin the elder (*c* 1470). Here the profile of Pythagoras' lute is based, like Arnaut's design, upon circles and small whole numbers. In contrast to Arnaut's lute, however, no 'cheating' is necessary in this case, as the so-called 'pythagorean triangle' marked out with X's in Figure 27 – a right triangle in which the length of the hypotenuse is 5 – guarantees the exact correspondence of geometric method and arithmetic result. The string length and the size and position of the rose are derived from the same

6 Alberti 1485 edition: y ii^v (book IX, ch. 5).   7 Baron 1727: 90.
8 Mersenne 1636-7: III, 50.

Figure 26. Syrlin's portrayal (*c*1470) of 'Pictagorus musice inventor'.

Appendix 4

module as the 3:4:5 triangle.[9] (This is of course the triangle which most simply embodies the 'pythagorean theorem', since $3^2 + 4^2 = 5^2$.)

One difficulty we face in studying the design of extant lutes from the sixteenth and seventeenth centuries is that these fragile objects have been subjected to the vicissitudes of time, often including refashionings as well as repairs, and we do not have the original stencils, specifications or the like. Our attempts to recover the original design would be hopelessly speculative if the instruments were merely constructed with the help of any old geometrical device;[10] but fortunately, many lutes embody simple ratios as required by the doctrine of proportion, and this gives us a more secure basis for conclusions about the builders' intentions.

Figure 28 shows the outline of the main part of a *liuto attiorbato* (for simplicity I have omitted the *tiorba* neck) built by Matteo Sellas at Venice *c*1640. In this case, so many measurements are multiples of the Venetian

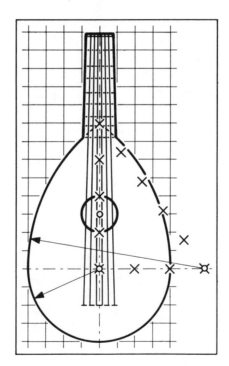

Figure 27. Mathematical design of the lute shown in Figure 26.

9   I have depicted a (pythagorean) fretting in order to show that the neck meets the body at fret 8, as it often does in early-sixteenth-century depictions of lutes (see Sommer 1920, nos. 10, 20, 23).
10   Edwards 1973; Abbott and Segerman 1976; Samson 1981.

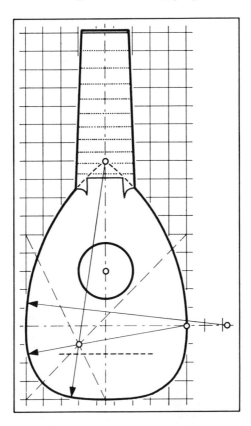

Figure 28. Geometrical design of the main part of Sellas' *liuto attiorbato* (*c*1640). The label reads 'Matteo Sellas alla [corona] in Venetia'.

inch that a chance coincidence would be most unlikely. According to Dours-ther's dictionary of weights and measures the Venetian inch was some 28.95-28.98 mm[11] (the modern inch is 25.4 mm). Using this unit of mea-sure we find that the diameter of the rose is rather exactly 3; the distance from the lower edge to the level of maximum width, 4; the distance to the centre of the rose, 7; the maximum width, 9; the length of the face, 12; the length of the capping strip, 15; the string length, $17\frac{1}{2}$; the length of the instrument with fingerboard, 20; and the length of the bass strings (not shown), 25 (7/10 of which are $17\frac{1}{2}$).

It is quite easy to construct the outline of Sellas' instrument by ruler and compass. The upper part is the same as in Syrlin's sculpture: as in Figure 27, the point outside the lute's outline lies to the right by 1/4 of its width (in

11   Or rather the foot some 347.4-347.74 mm. Doursther 1840: 418.

terms of the module, 1/4 of 9, or $2\frac{1}{4}$). The lower part of the outline (beneath the maximum width) is put together from circles whose centres lie, as shown, at the sides and top of the outline and at the intersection of two rudimentary diagonals. In renaissance treatises on architecture[12] these same diagonals were often used to demonstrate that ratios could be derived geometrically (see Figure 29), since the points of intersection of the diagonals and half-diagonals of a square divide it into nine equal squares. Thus in Figure 28, where the height and length of the large square is 9, that of the small square is 3.

The circles involved in Sellas' outline glide into each other. By means of the pythagorean theorem the radius of the largest circle can be derived from the instrument's maximum width as follows: $9 - \sqrt{6^2 + 1^2} + \sqrt{1.5^2 + 10^2} = 13.03$. By the modular construction it should be 13; hence the geometric and modular elements require much less 'tempering' than in Arnaut's lute.

For our final illustration let us consider a classical lute outline of the late sixteenth century. Three examples of this outline are to be found in the Vienna Sammlung alter Musikinstrumente: a seven-course tenor lute made by Vvendelio Venere in 1582 (see Figure 30); a lute originally made in

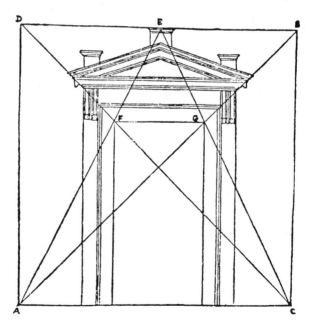

Figure 29. One of Serlio's proportional designs for a doorway (1551).

12   Alberti 1485 edition; Ryff 1547; Serlio 1551; Dietterlin 1598.

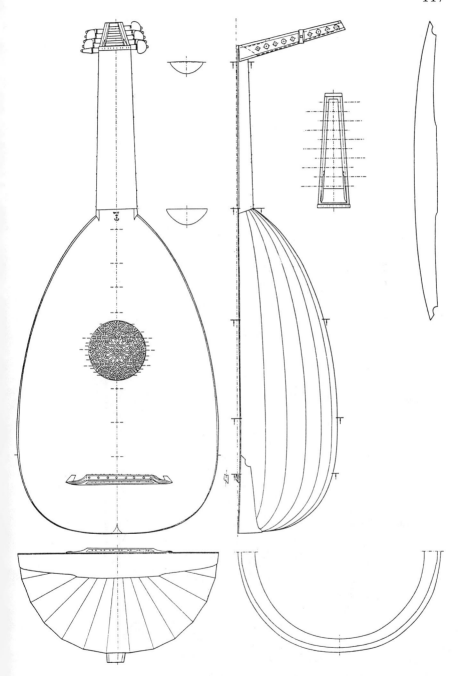

Figure 30. A tenor lute by Vvendelio Venere (1582).

1596 by Hanns Burkholtzer and later 'baroqued'; and an anonymous late-sixteenth-century mandora (perhaps originally a soprano lute?).

Figure 31 shows most of the modular elements. The diameter of the rose is 2; the distance from the bottom to the level of maximum width, 3; the distance up to the centre of the rose, 6; the maximum width, 7; the length of the capping strip, 10; the height of the outline figure, 11. The module is some 47 mm for the instruments by Venere and Burkholtzer, some 37 mm for the mandora.

Geometrically, the outline below the level of the maximum width can be constructed from circular arcs, much as in Figure 28. The rest of the outline, however, is not circular, but gradually bends more sharply as it rises. The curve is in fact elliptical. Ellipses were of great interest not only to Johannes Kepler (for the planetary orbits) but also to renaissance artists

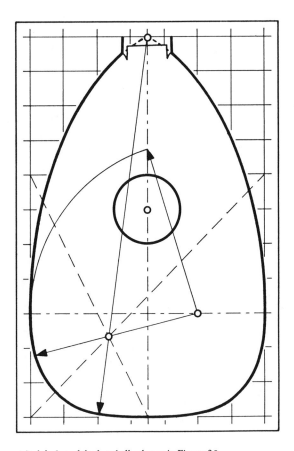

Figure 31. Geometrical design of the lute belly shown in Figure 30.

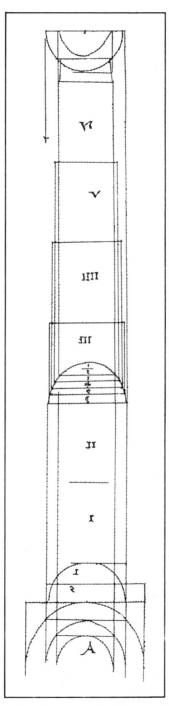

Figure 32. Dietterlin's illustration of a column whose sides follow an elliptical curve (1598).

(inasmuch as a circle drawn in perspective from a tilt appears elliptical) and early-baroque architects.[13] Among the various methods for constructing an ellipse perhaps the most practicable for a lute-maker would have been the one which Wendel Dietterlin (to cite one contemporary demonstration) used in his *Architectura* of 1598 to quantify the entasis or slight curvature in the shaft of a column, which prevents the illusion of concavity that a cylindrical column would produce (see Figure 32). In Figure 33 the same geometrical method is applied to the upper part of the outline in Figure 31. Point P (2 units from the opposite edge of the outline at its maximum width) is the centre of the circle from which the elliptical curve is derived by first dividing AI and A′I′ into equal parts (A′I′ being given as 8 modular units); then marking the points along the circle which lie directly to the left of the equidistant points along AI; and finally moving directly up to the level of the corresponding points on A′I′.

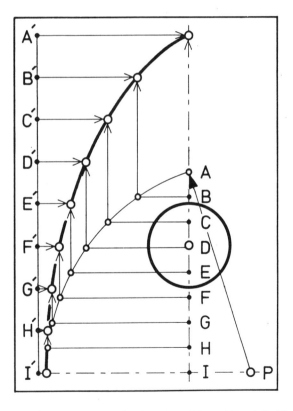

Figure 33. Application of Dietterlin's method to the outline of Venere's lute belly (Figure 31).

13 See Panofsky 1954.

I have confined myself to the analysis of some relatively simple designs because in these a chance coincidence between the original instrument and the mathematical reconstruction is most unlikely. My experience in examining historical lutes has been that the front profile lends itself readily to this kind of analysis in about one out of three cases. (A significant number of these instruments are by Hans Frei or Vvendelio Venere or from the workshop of Matteo Sellas.) The other instruments are too poorly preserved, or were conceived in so complicated a fashion that several interpretations are possible, or were designed without any mathematical method (e.g. Michielle Harton).

Unlike the lute depicted in Figure 26, nearly all the extant instruments which lend themselves to mathematical analysis do *not* embody the ratios most familiar to renaissance music theory, but favour ratios involving prime numbers higher than 2, 3 and 5. (In Figure 31, for instance, the ratio of width to length is 7:11.) This may perhaps have been due to a desire not to give preferential treatment to any note in the musical scale: pythagoreans were always poor at discriminating between materially significant and insignificant numerical coincidences. Even more fascinating, however, is the attempt, apparent in many designs, to bring geometric and arithmetic principles of construction into conformity notwithstanding some slight, mathematically inescapable discrepancies – rather like the commas which are dealt with in tempered tuning.

Works cited

Abbreviations:
DSB: *Dictionary of scientific biography*, ed. C. C. Gillespie (New York, 1970-80)
JLSA: *Journal of the Lute Society of America*
JVdGSA: *Journal of the Viola da Gamba Society of America*
LSJ: *Lute Society Journal*
New Grove: *The new Grove dictionary of music and musicians*, ed. S. Sadie (London, 1980)

[anonymous] 1974 facsimile edition: The Burwell Lute Tutor (Leeds)
——— 1556: *Discours non plus melancoliques que diverses . . .* (Poitiers)
——— *c*1665: manuscript criticism of John Berchinshaw (British Library Add. MS 4388)
——— 1899 edition: The Fitzwilliam Virginal Book (London)
Abbott, Djilda and Ephraim Segerman 1976: *The geometric description and analysis of instrument shapes* (Fellowship of Makers and Restorers of Historical Instruments, *Communication* 5)
Agricola, Martin 1545: *Musica instrumentalis deudsch* (4th edition, Wittenberg; diplomatic facsimile edition 1896: Publikationen alterer praktischer und theoretischer Musik-Werke, xx)
Alberti, Leon Battista 1485 edition: *De re aedificatoria* (Florence)
Anderson, Warren 1980: 'Musical developments in the school of Aristotle' (*Royal Musical Association Research chronicle* xvi, 78-98)
Anselmi, Giorgio 1961 edition: *De musica* (Florence)
Apel, Willi 1942: *The notation of polyphonic music, 900-1600* (Cambridge, Mass.)
Aristoxenus 1562 translation: *Harmonicorum elementorum libri III* (Venice)
——— 1902 edition with translation: *The harmonics of Aristoxenus* (Oxford)
Arnaut de Zwolle, Henri 1932 edition: *Les traités d'Henri-Arnaut de Zwolle . . .* (Paris)
Artusi, Giovanni Maria 1600: *L'Artusi . . . ragionamenti due* (Venice)
——— 1603: *Considerationi musicali* (Venice, bound with his *Seconda parte dell'Artusi* of the same year)
——— 1608: *Discorso secondo mvsicale di Antonio Braccino da Todi* (Venice)
Attaingnant, Pierre 1529: *Tres breue et familiere introduction . . .* (Paris)
Ban, Joan Albert 1643: *Kort zangh-bericht* (Amsterdam)
Barbieri, Patrizio 198-: *Acustica accordatura e temperamento nell'Illuminismo veneto* (Florence)
Barbour James Murray 1934: 'Nierop's hackebort' (*The musical quarterly* xx, 312-19)
——— 1951: *Tuning and temperament. A historical survey* (East Lansing)
Baron, Ernst Gottlieb 1727: *Historisch-theoretisch und practische Untersuchung des Instruments der Lauten* (Nuremberg)
Aron, Pietro 1516: *Libri tres de institutione harmonica* (Bologna)
——— 1545: *Lucidario in musica* (Venice)

Bartolus, Abraham 1614: 'Musica' (in H. Zeisung (ed.), *Theatri machinarum*, vi, Leipzig)
Beethoven, Ludwig van 1907 edition: *Beethovens sämtliche Briefe, kritische Ausgabe*, ii (Berlin and Leipzig)
Bermudo, Juan 1555: . . . *Declaración de instrumentos musicales* (Ossuna)
Biscargui: *see* Martinez de Biscargui
Boethius [c 500]: *De arithmetica*
—— [c 500]: *De institutione musica*
—— 1491 edition: *Musica* (Venice)
Bol, Hans 1973: *La basse de viole au temps de Marin Marais et d'Antoine Forqueray* (Bilthoven)
Bottrigari, Ercole 1599: *Il desiderio . . .* (Bologna)
Boyvin, Jacques 1675: *Premier livre d'orgue* (Paris)
Briggs, Henry 1624: *Arithmetica logarithmetica* (London)
[Brouncker, William] 1653: *Animadversions upon the Musick-compendium of Renat. Descartes* (London, bound with his translation of Descartes' *Musicae compendium*)
Burzio, Nicola 1487: *Musices opusculum* (Bologna)
Cardano, Girolamo 1570: *Opvs novvm de proportionibvs nvmerorvm* (Basel)
—— 1663 edition: *Operum tomus decimus* (London)
Clercx, Suzanne 1955: 'Johannes Ciconia théoricien' (*Annales musicologiques* iii: 39-75)
Couperin, Louis 1936 edition: *Oeuvres complètes* [sic] (Paris)
Damann, Rolf 1969: 'Die *Musica mathematica* von Bartolus' (*Archiv für Musikwissenschaft* xxvi, 140-62)
Danoville, 'Le Sieur' 1687: *L'art de toucher le dessus et basse de violle* (Paris)
Dart, Thurston 1958: 'Miss Mary Burwell's instruction book for the lute' (*Galpin Society Journal* xi, 3-62)
Denis, Jean 1650: *Traité de l'accord de l'espinette* (2nd edition, Paris)
Dietterlin, Wendel 1598: *Architectura . . .* (Nuremberg)
Dombois, Eugen 1974: 'Varieties of meantone temperament realized on the lute' (*JLSA* vii, 82-89)
—— 1980: 'Die Temperatur für Laute bei Hans Gerle . . .' (*Forum musicologicum*, ii, 60-71)
Doni, Giovanni Battista 1640: *Annotazioni sopra il Compendio de' generi* (Rome)
—— 1647: *De praestantia musicae veteris* (Florence)
—— 1763a edition: *Lyra barberina* [i] (Florence)
—— 1763b edition: *De' trattati di musica . . . tomo secondo* (Florence)
Doursther, Horace 1840: *Dictionnaire universelle des poids et mesures . . .* (Brussels)
Dowland, John 1974 edition: *Collected works* (London)
Dowland, Robert 1610: *Varietie of lute lessons* (London)
Dubbey, John 1970: 'Brouncker, William' (*DSB*)
Edwards, David 1973: 'A geometrical construction for a lute profile' (*LSJ* xv, 48-9)
Estève, M. 1755: 'Essai sur le meilleur système de musique harmonique, & sur son meilleur temperament' (*Mémoires de mathematique et de physique . . . de l'Académie Royale des Sciences*)
Euclid 1482 edition: *Preclarissimus liber elementorum . . .* (Venice)
Faulhaber, Johannes 1630: *Ingenieurs-Schul . . .* (Frankfurt)
Fine, Oronce 1530: *Epithoma musice instrumentalis* (Paris)
Fogliani, Ludovico 1529: *Musica theorica* (Venice)
Fritz, Barthold 1756: *Anweisung, wie man Claviere . . . nach ein mechanischen Art, in allen zwölf Tönen rein stimmen könne* (Leipzig)
Fuller, David 1976: 'French harpsichord playing in the 17th century – after Le Gallois' (*Early music* iv, 22-26)

Gafurio, Franchino 1496: *Practica musicae* (Milan)
—— 1518: *De harmonia musicorum instrumentorum opus* (Milan)
Galilei, Vincenzo 1581: *Dialogo . . . della musica antica et della moderna* (Venice)
—— 1584: *Fronimo . . .* (2nd edition, Venice)
Ganassi, Silvestro 1543: *Lettione seconda* (Venice)
Geoffroy, Jean-Nicolas posthumous manuscript: Livre des pièces de clavessin (Paris, Bibliothèque Nationale, MS Rés. 475)
Gerle, Hans 1532: *Musica teutsch* (Nuremberg)
—— 1533: *Tabulatur auff die Laudten* (Nuremberg)
Grayson, Cecil and Giulio Carlo Argon 1960: 'Alberti, Leon Battista' (*Dizionario biografico degli italiani*)
Hamm, P. 1975: 'Fine, Oronce' (*Dictionnaire de biographie française*)
Harwood, Ian 1960: 'A fifteenth century lute design' (*LSJ* ii, 3-8)
—— 1962: *Ten easy pieces for lute* (Cambridge)
—— : *see also* Poulton
Heartz, Daniel 1964: *Preludes, chansons and dances for lute* (Neuilly-sur-Seine)
Heinze, Johann Jakob Wilhelm 1795-6: *Hildegard von Hohenthal* (Berlin)
Hummel, Johann Nepomuk 1827: *Ausführliche theoretisch-practische Anweisung zum Piano-forte-Spiel* (Vienna and London)
—— 1828 translation: *A complete and practical course . . .* (London)
Husmann, Heinrich 1967: 'Zur Characteristik der Schlickschen Temperatur' (*Archiv für Musikwissenschaft* xxiv, 253-65)
Jahnal, Franz 1962: *Die Guitarre und ihr Bau* (Frankfurt)
Juschkewitsch, A.P. 1964: *Geschichte der Mathematik im Mittelalter* (Leipzig)
Kircher, Athanasius 1650: *Musurgia universalis* (Rome)
Lanfranco, Giovanni Maria 1533: *Scintille di musica* (Brescia)
Le Blanc, Hubert 1740: *Defense de la basse de viole* (Amsterdam)
Lefèvre, Jacques 1496: *. . . Musica libris demonstrata quattuor*; (or) *. . . Elementa musicalia* (Paris)
Legrenze, Johannes 1876 edition: *Ritus canendi vetustissimus et novus* (in E. de Coussemaker (ed.), Scriptorum de musica medii aevi novam seriem iv, Paris, 298-420)
Levitan, Joseph S. 1936-8: 'Adrian Willaert's famous duo *Quidnam ebrietas . . .*' (*Tijdschrift der Vereeniging voor Nederlandsche Muziekgeschiedenis* xv, 166-233)
Lindley, Mark 1974: 'Early 16th-century keyboard temperaments' (*Musica disciplina* xxviii, 129-51)
—— 1975-6: 'Fifteenth-century evidence for meantone temperament' (*Proceedings of the Royal Musical Association* cii, 37-51)
—— 1977: 'Instructions for the clavier diversely tempered' (*Early music* v, 18-23)
—— 1980a: 'Pythagorean intonation and the rise of the triad' (*Royal Musical Association Research chronicle* xvi, 4-61)
—— 1980b: 'Mersenne on keyboard tuning' (*Journal of music theory* xxiv, 167-204)
—— 1980c: Temperaments' (*New Grove*)
—— 198–: 'Stimmung und Temperatur' (in F. Zaminer (ed.), *Geschichte der Musiktheorie*, vi)
Lowinsky, Edward E. 1956-8: 'Adrian Willaert's chromatic "duo" re-examined' (*Tijdshrift voor muziekwetenschap* xviii, 1-36)
Macran, Henry S. 1902: *see* Aristoxenus
Macrobius 1848 edition: *Opera*, i (Quedlinberg and Leipzig)
Marais, Marin 1686: *Pieces à vne et à deux violes* (Paris)
—— 1689: *Basse-continües des pieces à une et à deux violes* (Paris)
—— c1976 edition: *Six suites for viol and thoroughbass* (Madison)

Marchetto of Padua 1784 edition: *Lucidarium musicae planae* (in M. Gerbert (ed.), Scriptores ecclesiastici de musica sacra . . . III, St Blasien, 64-121)

Marpurg, Friedrich Wilhelm 1776: *Versuch über die musikalische Temperatur* (Breslau)

Marsden, Eric William 1971: *Greek and Roman artillery, technical treatises* (Oxford)

Martinez de Biscargui, Gonçalo 1528: *Arte de canto llano . . .* (5th edition, Burgos)

—— 1550: *Arte de canto llano . . .* (11th edition, Burgos)

Mersenne, Marin 1636-7: *Harmonie universelle* (Paris)

—— 1637b: *Nouvelles observations physiques et mathématiques* (appended to *Harmonie universelle* III, Paris)

—— 1932-: *Correspondance du P. Mersenne* (Paris)

Milán, Luis 1536: *Libro de musica de vihuela da mano, intitulado El maestro* (Valencia)

—— 1927 edition: *El maestro* (Leipzig)

Miller, Clement A. 1973: *Hieronymus Cardanus, Writings on music* (American Institute of Musicology)

Minnaert, M.G.J. 1976: 'Stevin, Simon' (*DSB*)

Monteverdi, Claudio 1603: *Il quarto libro de madrigali* (Venice)

—— 1605: *Il quinto libro de madrigali* (Venice)

—— 1609: *L'Orfeo, favola in musica* (Venice)

—— 1614: *Il sesto libro de madrigali* (Venice)

—— 1961 edition: *Lamento d'Arianna* (Florence)

Morley, Thomas 1597: *A plaine and easie introduction to practicall musicke* (London)

Münxelhaus, Barbara 1976: *Pythagoras musicus . . .* (Bonn)

Nassarre, Pablo 1723: *Escvela mvsica, segun la pratica moderna* (Saragossa)

Neidhardt, Johann Georg 1732: *Gantzlich erschöpfte, mathematische Abtheilungen . . .* (Königsberg and Leipzig)

Newton, Isaac [1665]: manuscript studies on music (Cambridge University Library Add. MS 4000)

van Nierop, Dyrck Rembrantz 1659: *Wiskonstige musyka* (Amsterdam, bound with his *Mathematische calculatie*)

Nivers, Guillaume-Gabriel 1675: *Troisième livre d'orgue* (Paris)

Ozanam, Jacques 1691: *Dictionnaire mathématique* (Amsterdam)

Palisca, Claude 1967: 'The *Musica* of Erasmus of Höritz' (in J. La Rue (ed.), *Aspects of mediaeval and renaissance music*, New York)

—— 1968: 'The Artusi-Monteverdi controversy' (in D. Arnold and N. Fortune (eds.), *The Monteverdi companion*, London)

—— 198-: 'Von Zarlino bis 1640' (in F. Zaminer (ed.), *Geschichte der Musiktheorie*, VII)

Panofsky, Erwin 1954: *Galileo as a critic of the arts* (The Hague)

Pierce, Jane Illingworth 1973: 'Hans Gerle: sixteenth century lutenist and pedagogue' (dissertation, Chapel Hill)

—— 1980: 'Finé, Oronce' (*New Grove*)

Podio, Guillermo de 1495: *Ars musicorum* (Valencia)

Poulle, Emmanuel 1978: 'Fine, Oronce' (*DSB*, supplement I)

Poulton, Diana 1972: *John Dowland, his life and times* (Berkeley and Los Angeles)

Poulton, Diana and Ian Harwood 1980: 'Lute' (*New Grove*)

Praetorius, Michael 1619: *Syntagma musicum*, II: *De organographia* (Wolfenbüttel)

Prosdocimo de' Beldemandi 1913 edition: 'Opusculum contra theoricam partem sive speculativam Lucidarii Marchetti patavini' (*Rivista musicale italiana* XX, 707-62)

Ptolemy 1562 translation: *Harmonicorum, seu de musica libri III* (Venice, bound with a translation of Aristoxenus)

Rameau, Jean-Philippe 1737: *Génération harmonique* (Paris)

Ramis de Pareja, Bartolomeo 1482: *Musica practica* (Bologna)

Razzi, Fausto 1980: 'Polyphony of the seconda prattica . . .' (*Early music* VIII, 298-312)

Reinhard, Andreas 1604: *Monochordum* (Leipzig)

Roche, Martine 1967: 'Un livre de clavecin français de la fin du XVIIe siècle' (*Recherches sur la musique classique française* VII, 39-73)

Rossi, Lemme 1666: *Sistema mvsico, overo musica speculativa* (Perugia)

Rousseau, Jean 1687: *Traité de la viole* (Paris)

Rousseau, Jean-Jacques 1768: *Dictionnaire de musique* (Paris)

Ryff, Walther Hermann 1547: *Der furnembsten, notwendigsten, der gantzen Architectur angehörigen mathematischen vnd mechanischen kunst* (Nuremberg)

Salinas, Francisco 1577: *De musica libri VII* (Salamanca)

Salmon, Thomas 1705: 'The theory of music reduced to arithmetical and geometrical proportions' (*Philosophical transactions of the Royal Society* XXIV)

Samson, W. 1981: *Lute outlines, a pragmatic approach to geometrical description* (Fellowship of makers and restorers of historical instruments, communication 377)

Sancta Maria, Tomas de 1565: *Arte de tañer fantasia* (Valladolid)

Sauveur, Joseph 1707: 'Methode générale pour former les systèmes tempérés de musique' (*Mémoires de mathématique et de physique . . . de l'Académie Royale des Sciences*)

Schlick, Arnolt 1511: *Spiegel der Orgelmacher vn Organisten* (Speyer)

—— 1512: *Tabulaturen etlicher lobgesang vnd lidlein . . .* (Mainz)

—— 1869 edition: 'Spiegel der Orgelmacher und Organisten' (*Monatshefte für Musikgeschichte* I, 77-114)

—— 1965 edition: *Tabulaturen . . . uff die lauten* (Die Tabulatur, III: Hofheim am Taunus)

Schreiber, Heinrich 1514: *Algorithmus proportionum vna cum monochordi generis dyatonici compositione* (Cracow)

—— 1518-21: *Ayn new kunstlich Buech* (Nuremberg)

Schubart, Christian Friedrich Daniel 1806: *Ideen zu einer Ästhetik der Tonkunst* (Vienna)

Segerman, Ephraim: *see* Abbott

Serlio, Sebastiano 1551: *Extraordinario libro di architettvra* (Lyon)

Sommer, Hermann 1920: *Die Laute . . . Eine Bildmonographie* (Berlin)

Spataro, Giovanni 1521: *Errori de Franchino Gafurio da Lodi* (Bologna)

Spencer, Robert 1976: 'Chitarrone, theorbo and archlute' (*Early music* IV, 404-22)

Stevin, Simon 1884 edition: *Vande spiegeling der singconst* (Amsterdam)

—— 1966 edition: *The principal works of Simon Stevin*, V (Amsterdam)

Strunk, Oliver 1950: *Source readings in music history* (Princeton)

Thompson, Thomas Perronet 1829: *Instructions to my daughter for playing the enharmonic guitar* (London)

Tilmouth, Michael 1980: 'Salmon, Thomas' (*New Grove*)

Valderrabano, Enriquez de 1547: *Libro de musica de vihuela, intitulado Silva de sirenas* (Valladolid)

—— 1965 edition: *. . . Silva de sirenas* (Barcelona)

Vicentino, Nicola 1555: *L'antica musica ridotta alla moderna prattica* (Rome)

Vitruvius *c* 1486 edition: *De architectura* (Rome)

Ward, John 1953: 'The vihuela da mano and its literature' (dissertation, New York)

Wright, Owen 1980: 'Arab music' (*New Grove*)

Zarlino, Gioseffo 1558: *Istitutione harmoniche* (Venice)

—— 1571: *Dimostrationi harmoniche* (Venice)

—— 1588: *Sopplimenti musicali* (Venice)

Index